Life Uploaded

Life Uploaded

Sierra Furtado

GALLERY BOOKS
New York London Toronto Sydney New Delhi

Gallery Books
An Imprint of Simon & Schuster, Inc.
1230 Avenue of the Americas
New York, NY 10020

This book is a work of fiction. Any references to historical events, real people, or real places are used fictitiously. Other names, characters, places, and events are products of the author's imagination, and any resemblance to actual events or places or persons, living or dead, is entirely coincidental.

A Beaufresh Book

First Gallery Books hardcover edition October 2016

GALLERY BOOKS and colophon are registered trademarks of Simon & Schuster, Inc.

For information about special discounts for bulk purchases, please contact Simon & Schuster Special Sales at 1-866-506-1949 or business@simonandschuster.com.

The Simon & Schuster Speakers Bureau can bring authors to your live event. For more information or to book an event contact the Simon & Schuster Speakers Bureau at 1-866-248-3049 or visit our website at www.simonspeakers.com.

Manufactured in the United States of America

10 9 8 7 6 5 4 3 2 1

Library of Congress Cataloging-in-Publication Data

ISBN 978-1-5011-4395-3
ISBN 978-1-5011-4398-4 (ebook)

To all my #Sierranators out there—
if you are reading this, you are perfect.

Life Uploaded

PROLOGUE

Once Upon a Time

Once upon a time, not so long ago, there was an awkward, nervous middle school girl—that's me!—who wanted nothing more than to be invisible. Okay, that's a lie; I wanted a little bit more than that. I wanted Jack Walsh. Jack was not the cutest or the coolest guy in school, but he was the only guy in school, as far as I was concerned. He had dark hair, deep amber eyes, and soft lips I couldn't help but want, want, *want*. He read Steinbeck and played a baby-blue Stratocaster—I know, I *know*, but I was only thirteen, okay? Most important, he had this intensity when he spoke to me, as if I were the only person he'd ever want to speak to as long as he lived, and that made me feel . . . spectacular.

The problem was, I wasn't the only person he wanted to speak to. Nor was I the only girl he spoke to with such intensity. Actually, as it turned out (to my total and complete dismay), he was madly in love with my best friend Gwendolyn Crane, whom I'd known since kindergarten. I didn't blame him. Gwen was tall and blond with immaculate skin and electrifying green eyes. She could quote lines from *Pretty Little Liars* (her bible), she followed bands I'd never even heard of, and at only thirteen years old, she could have competed in the Olympics of flirting. And taken home the gold. Yes, I know that's not a real thing, but Gwen was just that smooth.

Then there was me: gangly and uncoordinated, brown hair, greenish grayish eyes, my once adorable baby face completely disrupted by braces, which might as well have been a mouth full of barbed wire. I stumbled over my words as much as I stumbled over my feet. Sure, I had my blue eyes, but those were less appealing when hidden behind horn-rimmed glasses. Boys made me blush (not in a cute way), and girls made me cry (they were cruel even then). Long story short: I was a graceless bundle of nerves, a completely unviable romantic choice when there were Gwendolyn Cranes roaming the earth. So like I said, I didn't blame him for falling for her instead of me (like he was supposed to), and I didn't blame her for falling for him (did I mention he was perfect? I guess Gwen thought so, too). They made a great couple, everyone said so.

So I decided to bury my feelings and get on board the Gwen and Jack train, no matter how much it hurt, as any good best friend would. I spent all of seventh and eighth grade watching them hold hands and kiss in the quad when they thought no one was watching. I listened as Gwen confided in me their tour of all the bases with details so sharp and crisp it was like my brain was a chalkboard and her words were nails, painted red and sharpened to a point (first base in an alley while walking home from school, second base in her bedroom with the door cracked open, her parents watching Oprah downstairs). I listened when she called me crying about fights they'd had (once he'd kissed another girl during gym and then confessed to her, for example), and each time I'd pray they'd break up and then hate myself for it. I also hated how much I loved the conversations I had with him during orchestra (he played the cello, I played the violin, and Gwen played nothing, so this was the only alone time I had with Jack). We'd be putting away our music stands at the end of class and he'd throw his arms around me and say, "How's your day, my beautiful Harper?" I'd smile and tell him about my classes, too swept off my feet to mention that I was in no way *his*, despite wanting to be, or that I knew he was only calling me beautiful to make me feel less insecure about my braces, or that I knew for a fact his girlfriend did not like when he called other girls beautiful, regardless of his reasoning or motive.

I worried every day that I was a terrible friend for harboring these all-consuming feelings for my best friend's boyfriend, and then one day this worry was confirmed by Gwen herself, who screamed it at me while staining her shirt with dark and inky mascara tears.

See, I had also written down everything I'm telling you now in a diary, plus a whole lot of other super private thoughts and emotions that absolutely no one was ever allowed to read, not even my best friend—especially not her. But on this particular Wednesday (just six days away from junior high graduation), Gwen came over to my house after school. While I was in the bathroom, she took the liberty of snooping through my desk and reading said secret diary. When I returned to my room she threw the book at my head.

"I knew it!" she screamed. "I've always known you liked him, I just didn't want to admit it to myself. I told myself you were too good of a friend to betray me. I can't believe this!"

"Gwen . . ." I shut the door behind me and picked up the diary, trying to stay calm even as I felt my heart would explode out of my chest. "They're just feelings that I have, okay? I've never done anything about them, and I never would. I've been trying to get rid of this . . . crush, or whatever it is, because the last thing I'd ever want is to mess up your relationship. That's my private diary. You were never supposed to—"

"But I just *knew* that you were hiding something from me and I couldn't stand it anymore. I had to read it. Otherwise I'd never know for sure."

"And you couldn't have just *asked* me?"

"You would have lied!"

"Fine. Well, I'm telling you the truth now. I've liked Jack for a long time, but I'm your friend and I'll never do anything about it. Ever."

"And I'm telling you the truth now: you're an amazing liar and a horrible friend. All this time I've been confiding in you, thinking I could trust you?! How stupid was I? Get out of my way." She pushed me aside and reached for the doorknob.

"Where are you going?"

"Home." Her voice was hard, her tone wooden. "I never want to see you again. I hope you and Jack are very happy together."

"Gwen! You're overreacting; he doesn't even like me. He sees me as a friend. He loves you! You have nothing to be worried about!" But she wasn't listening; instead, she was bounding down our stairs and out the front door, leaving a trail of Marc Jacobs perfume as she went.

I didn't know it then, but this would be the last sight I would have of Gwendolyn Crane for a long time: pouting on my street corner, blond hair shining in the sunlight, pacing for a few minutes before her mom's black Range Rover pulled up to the curb and swooped her away.

One year later I had gone from being an awkward middle schooler to being an awkward freshman in high school. The only real differences were that Gwen and Jack broke up after she transferred to Malibu High (it was closer to where she lived and was an easy way to never see me), my braces came off, and I made a small group of friends: three girls, all named Jessica. They went by Jessie, Jessa, and Jess (I swear on my life, you can't make this stuff up), and invited me to sit with them at lunch on the first day of freshman year after Mrs. Chapman, the geometry teacher, accidentally read my middle name instead of my first name during roll call. So what's my middle name? If you guessed Jessica, you are correct. The Jessicas were disappointed to learn my actual first name, but they were sweet girls and insisted I keep eating lunch with them regardless. So I spent the next few months living a very low-key, regular, *calm* existence, going to classes, eating lunch with the Jessicas, and walking a certain path around campus that would maximize my chances of bumping into Jack Walsh.

And sometimes I would succeed. I'd time it perfectly so that I'd walk past his math class just as he was leaving, and he'd smile and give me a hug before we'd walk across campus to his next class in the science building, laughing about whatever. As soon as he'd enter his classroom, I'd turn right around and power-walk back in the other direction to where *my* next class was, in the language building. By the time the bell rang I'd be panting and out of breath, but it was always worth it. For quite a while I felt guilty for being unable to stop harboring these feelings toward my best friend's ex-boyfriend. Sure, she had moved schools and wasn't speaking to me, but we had been close for so long that I just assumed we would work it out. But after months of my texting and calling and emailing her with nothing but radio silence in response, I realized she intended to cut me out for good. And if she didn't want to know me anymore, shouldn't I be allowed to let my crush on Jack run wild? As if I even had a choice in the matter. I often caught myself daydreaming about his finally asking me out. I hoped that Gwen being out of the picture would allow him to finally realize, Taylor Swift style, that he belonged with me. But alas, he never did.

Then came the day that changed everything. It was a Monday, and I was dawdling in the downstairs hallway of the math building, taking my time so that I'd cross Mr. Contreras's class at the exact moment Jack normally walked out of it. This was usually about three minutes after the bell rang (he was slow at packing up, I knew this), but sometimes it was two minutes and sometimes it was four; there was no way to know for sure. I'm not, and have never been, a mind reader.

On this day Jack emerged from the classroom a magic three minutes after the bell rang, and we practically bumped into each other in the hallway. Perfect.

"Harper!" He put his hand on my hip before continuing to speak, "I love how I always run into you right after math. Honestly, the highlight of my day."

"Oh, please." I blushed. "Anyway, how's your day?"

"Well, it was kind of lame, but now you're here, so I have nothing to complain about."

"Aw, you're a sweetheart," I said as we walked out of the math building and onto the main quad. There must have been a hint of sarcasm or bitterness or *something* in my voice, because then he said, "What? What's wrong?"

"What do you mean? Why would something be wrong?"

"You seem . . . sad. Or annoyed. I can't tell which. Maybe both?"

"Nope. Neither," I lied. "I'm totally fine."

"Are you sure? Because you know I'm your friend and you can tell me anything. I feel like we used to talk all the time and then suddenly—I know things got kind of weird with Gwen, and then she left out of nowhere, and yes, that totally sucked for both of us, but I don't see why that should mean you and I can't talk like we used to. I miss you, you know? I miss our conversations."

"Yeah, I do too." I chewed the inside of my cheek, contemplating whether I should say what I'd been dying to say for over a year and a half.

"Yeah? So then what's going on, Harp?"

I broke down. "Okay, here's the thing." I launched right in. "I've always felt that you and I have a really strong connection." I was unstoppable. "I think you're . . . incredible. To be completely honest, I think about you all the time. I've thought about you pretty much since the day I met you."

"Harper, I—"

"Wait, let me finish. When Gwen left, I thought maybe finally you'd see that we could be together. I thought maybe you'd realize it was me you wanted all along and you'd ask me out, so yeah, if I seem sad and annoyed, it's because you just haven't. And I'm starting to get that you never will."

"Oh boy." He took a deep breath. "Are you finished now?"

"Uh . . . yes." I felt light with relief; the burden of these secret feelings had been lifted.

"Okay. Listen, Harper, I love you. You're so special to me, and you always have been. And you always will be. But I don't feel . . . that way about you."

The world crashed down around me, splinters of my pride and dignity flying every which way. I couldn't believe what I was hearing. For a year and a half I'd dreaded telling Jack how I felt out of fear that he'd reject me. I'd had nightmares about this very moment, and now it was actually happening.

"Harper? Are you okay?"

"I'm fine," I snapped, feeling pale as a ghost and just as fragile.

"You don't have feelings for me, I get it. I guess I'm not surprised—no, you know what? I am surprised. You've always been extra sweet to me, and you're more than just friendly. For as long as I remember, you've gone out of your way to flirt with me. So that was all, what? An act? For what? To make Gwen jealous?"

"It wasn't an act!" he protested. "Listen, I love you—but just as a really, really great friend, Harp. I'm sorry if something I did made you think . . . something else."

"I have to get to class," I said, blinking extra fast to keep from crying.

"I really hope we can still be friends, Harp."

"I, uh . . . I have to get to class," I repeated, having nothing else to say, and hurried out of sight as quickly as my feet could carry me.

That day after school when my mom picked me up, I jumped into her Volkswagen SUV and burst out crying. Big fat tears rolled down my cheeks, the kind that fall so hard they get in your mouth and your hair. Salt water *everywhere*.

"Baby!" My mom turned around, horrified. "What's the matter?"

In between sobs and gasps for air I tried to explain to her what had happened. I sounded like a dying chinchilla (I think? Not that I know the first thing about what a dying chinchilla sounds like), but after a while she was able to put the pieces together.

She seemed relieved. "Ah, so it begins."

"So *what* begins?" I sobbed.

"The heartbreaking adolescent years. This is all very normal stuff, Harpy. Any teenage girl worth her salt will get her heart broken at least once. As far as I'm concerned, you're not a real teenager until you've had your first heartbreak."

"Uggghhhhh," I groaned, truly in agony. "I never want to feel this again. Ever! I'm humiliated, Mom. How am I supposed to show my face around him now? And what if he tells people? Everyone is just going to feel sorry for me and think I'm this sad, pathetic, little loser."

"No, they absolutely will not think that."

"They will!"

"Listen to me, Harper. They won't."

"Why not?"

"You'll see." She turned the car around and drove us in silence to the Santa Monica mall. She pulled into the parking lot and turned off the car. "Look," she said, "when I was your age and I'd get sad over a boy, my mom would always say, 'The best revenge is looking fabulous,' and she'd take me on a shopping spree. Now, that may not be the best parenting, but it's what we're going to do. Come on, let's do some damage."

I'm not going to lie to you, that day we shopped 'til we dropped. And then we shopped some more. By the time we got home, it was nine at night and my legs were so sore I thought they might fall off. I had more than enough gorgeous new outfits to help me play the part of Girl Who Actually Doesn't Care That You Rejected Her, and was beginning to realize that the humiliation of being rejected wasn't fatal. I could be rejected and still be awesome. I could still be beautiful and totally fierce. That doesn't mean the brutal sting of today's events was any less painful, but at least then I knew I had it in me to recover.

I ate a late dinner with my parents and then retreated to my bedroom. The events of the day had left my mind reeling, and I didn't feel totally ready for bed, so I did what I always do when there's nothing better to do (and sometimes even when there is something better to do): I logged on to Facebook.

Now, I don't know if the decision to log on to Facebook in that moment is what changed my life completely and forever, but it definitely played a role. Sometimes I wonder how things might have been different if I hadn't gone to my Facebook page that night and seen that one of the Jessicas (the one who went by Jess) had posted a YouTube video made by a girl named Cynthia Watson. The video was called "How to Do Your Makeup Like a Heartbreaker," so I clicked on it, thinking the only thing missing from my drop-dead outfit for tomorrow would be some heartbreaker makeup, whatever that was. I watched mesmerized from beginning to end while Cynthia Watson went through the motions of covering up blemishes, applying smoky cat eyes, contouring cheekbones, and plumping up lips using lip liner and gloss. She made it all look so easy . . . and really, really fun.

The only problem was I didn't have any of the products she used in my arsenal (I didn't even *have* a makeup arsenal, to be honest), so I went downstairs and asked my mom if I could borrow some.

"Aren't you a little too young for makeup?" she asked.

"I got my heart broken today, Mom, that means I'm officially a teenager. You said so yourself."

She had to agree, and soon I was watching Cynthia's video again, this time practicing on myself as she went through the steps. When I was finished, I looked more like a clown than a heartbreaker, but I didn't care; I washed it off and tried again. Cynthia's video led to other videos, and those videos led to more videos, all about makeup techniques and hairstyles and sometimes fashion tips. I lost track of time, watching one after the other. I stayed up all night like this, and by the time morning came, it felt as though I'd watched every beauty tutorial YouTube had to offer. The truth is, I'd only just scratched the tip of the iceberg.

It was seven in the morning and I was exhausted but too excited to notice. I had discovered a whole new world, and I had a heartbreaking ensemble to wear that would surely blow Jack out of the water. I felt like a completely new girl, ready to flaunt my new look and break some hearts.

I showed up to school wearing high-waisted jeans, a white halter top, and suede high-heeled booties. For the first time in my life I was wearing a full face of makeup, and the feeling was exhilarating. I had spent hours during the night imagining what it would be like to talk to Jack when I saw him, but I hadn't considered everyone else in the school. I hadn't considered that going from overalls to halter tops overnight would take me from being invisible to, well, quite visible. People stared as I walked down the halls like I was Sandy in the last scene of *Grease*. People who I'd never spoken to before said things like "Wow, Harper, you look . . . different," and "Oh my god, I *love* your outfit." I had been so worried that everyone would find out about my being rejected and feel sorry for me, but I flipped the script! If people had found out, it didn't matter now, because I had given them something better to talk about, and in *this* conversation, I wasn't a reject. Funny how I'd always wanted to be invisible and left alone. I never knew being noticed would feel *so much better*.

When I did finally see Jack, it happened naturally. I didn't walk past his class and I didn't look around for him. In between Spanish and world history, I stopped at the vending machines to buy a pack of Chips Ahoy!. I bent down to grab them from the dispenser, and when I stood back up, there was Jack, looking pretty nervous and fairly uncomfortable.

"Oh God, you scared me." I gripped my snack, slightly crushing the cookies, but stayed cool.

"Sorry," he said, "I didn't mean to."

"That's okay."

"So, how're you doing?"

"Me? I'm great, why?"

"Well, you look great. I like your, uh . . . everything, actually, the whole thing looks great."

"Thanks."

"I just wanted to make sure you're all right and that you're not, like, horribly mad at me or anything."

"Mad? No, I'm not mad. You were right, Jack, we're not a good match, I just didn't see it until you pointed it out. I'm glad we're going to be just friends."

"Oh. Really? That's awesome. I'm so relieved!"

"Yay." I gave him my sweetest smile, while keeping my tone dry and unenthusiastic.

"So, wanna see a movie after school?"

"I can't today, sorry."

"What about tomorrow?"

"Hmm, I'll check my schedule. See ya around!" I kissed him casually on the cheek and headed to class, feeling like a million dollars. No, *five* million dollars. I was finally taking my life into my own hands.

Now, let me make one thing clear for anybody reading this who might one day follow in my footsteps: the clothes and makeup themselves did not change how I felt about myself, they just helped me to unleash the power that had been inside me all along. Remember in *The Wizard of Oz* how the ruby slippers represented Dorothy's inner ability to get herself home that she had all along but never knew? It's like that.

At lunch, the Jessicas' mouths hung open.

"Harper, you look . . ." Jessie started.

"Let me guess?" I said. "Different."

"Exquisite!" Jessa jumped in.

"Thank you, guys! I'm so happy you like."

"Don't take this the wrong way, but what *happened*?" Jess asked.

"Well, actually, I watched that video you posted on Facebook. The Cynthia Watson one."

"Isn't she great?"

"Yes! I learned so much! And there are so many other videos out there, I had no idea. It's a gold mine!"

"Oh, yeah, YouTube tutorials? It's definitely becoming a thing," said Jessa.

"I don't really get it, to be honest," said Jessie. "Random girls make videos about how to do makeup for different occasions and I'm supposed to just trust them? Who are they to tell me what to put on my face?"

"So cynical!" said Jess. "It's not like that. These girls have something to share, so they're sharing it. You don't *have* to listen to them, but there are plenty of girls out there who want a solid teacher in that department. And Cynthia Watson delivers!"

The gears in my head started to turn. I thought about how empowered I'd felt all day, how good it felt to take my look and my confidence into my own hands, and I wanted to share that with anyone who would listen. What if there was another girl like me out there whose heart got broken? What if she found a video I made and it changed how she felt about herself? What if, at only fourteen and a half years old, I could make a difference? I knew that the first lesson of beauty is that it's only skin deep, but maybe I could use it as a way to help girls find confidence. The idea was exhilarating.

That day when I got home I made my first YouTube video: "Three Outfits to Boost Your Mood." And that, my friends, is the story of how I went from living life to living life, uploaded.

TWO YEARS LATER

TUTORIAL #1

New Year's Eve Makeup, Outfit Ideas, and DIY Photo Booth!

Hi everyone! Harper here! What is up?!

Today's video is all about New Year's Eve! It's right around the corner, and as you can tell, I am very excited about it! SUPER pumped.

I thought it would be cool to show you guys some last-minute outfit ideas along with some makeup inspiration and also a do-it-yourself photo booth kind of thing, ya know? No? You don't know? Just keep an open mind, you're gonna love this one, I swear.

So leave your comments below telling me what your New Year's resolutions are going to be! I think mine is to eat less dairy. If you know me at all, you know I love milk, like, so much. But recently I stayed up until three in the morning just watching scary videos about the dairy industry and now I'm kinda scarred, basically. So here's to a year of no dairy! Or less dairy. Hopefully.

First off, I'm going to show you what to do for your New Year's Eve makeup. I thought of this really super easy look that I will probably be wearing myself.

1. Start off with a layer of foundation. Then just use some concealer to smooth out any blemishes or uneven areas.

2. Next, use a concealer to highlight your face—nose, forehead, under your eyes. This will make you look more awake, which is important because you gotta stay up late on New Year's Eve! Then blend it all in—starting from the center of your face and working outward—with a beauty blender sponge. If you don't know what that is, it's one of those squishy foam wedges that you use to make sure all your makeup has been applied evenly. I honestly couldn't live life without 'em.
3. Next, dip a fluffy brush into your favorite loose powder and tap the handle of the brush against your wrist a few times to shake off any excess. Sweep the powder all around your eyes to make them shine!
4. If you'd like, you can apply pressed powder all over your face to set and secure everything you've done so far.
5. Time for eyebrows! I recommend an Anastasia brow pencil to fill in your brows and brush them out. This is one of my favorite things to do, and it literally takes me at least ten whole minutes. Seriously. If that's wrong, then I don't wanna be right. Before moving on, quickly smooth on some eyebrow gel to keep them in place throughout the night.
6. As for your eye shadow, I recommend using the Tartelette Amazonian clay matte palette by Tarte. This one is a very neutral palette, nothing too crazy—it's my freaking obsession. First, I apply free spirit—a light brown matte shade—as a base. Then I apply a shimmery light brown shade right on top of that (half baked by Urban Decay is *amaze*). Then blend multi-tasker or fashionista—aka the darkest matte brown shade in this palette—to create a shadow effect in the far corners. Add some highlighting cream to

the very top of your lids where they meet your brow bones. And BAM, just like that, your eyes are contoured.

7. Can't go out to a New Year's Eve party without some liquid eyeliner, now can you? I like to use liquid eyeliner by Kat Von D because IMHO (in my humble opinion) it's the easiest to put on. Also, cat eyes, anyone?
8. If you want your eyelash game to be super on point this New Year's Eve, I recommend some extensions. Just glue 'em on and apply mascara to blend them with your real eyelashes. Works like a charm. If you choose to go this route, don't forget to apply your liquid eyeliner after your lash extensions; that way, you can cover up any visible lash glue!
9. Moving on to the lips! My favorite part. First, line your lips with pencil; I like to use one by MAC named Whirl. Then pick a lipstick color (I'm going with Sydney by Buxom) and fill in the lines. Oooh, pretty!
10. Voilà, your makeup is complete!

Now, before we move on to the outfit ideas, I'm gonna show you an awesome way to celebrate (and take amazing Instagram photos) before you even leave the house. It's DIY photo booth time!

Head to the store and grab a bunch of decorations. Shimmery streamers for the wall and big gold balloons that write out the year are a must; these are your background. Then just go wild with whatever props you want: glittery glasses, party hats, boas, crowns—anything you can get your hands on, really. I know I will definitely be doing one of these this year. Then just strike a pose and go selfie-crazy!

Now, the moment you've all been waiting for: OUTFITS!

1. Outfit number one is a high-necked black crop top with silvery snowflakes on it, paired with a fringed black skirt from H&M. Finishing off the look are glittery tights and blue leather booties.
2. This next one is really cute, if I do say so myself. It's a rose-colored, sequined romper from Forever 21 paired with a furry black cardigan from Brandy Melville. I'd go ahead and pair it with some accessories like layered chokers, sheer black tights, and matching black booties.
3. If you're tryna wear something super chic, this outfit is for you. This gray faux fur coat is from Topshop, and so is the blue velvet romper to go with it! The romper has a really high collar that will actually wrap around your neck like a choker, but it also has a low V neck cut out for a little sexiness. If there's ever a night to dress sexy, that night is New Year's Eve.
4. The last outfit is super easy. It's just a jumpsuit, so literally one item of clothing, with black velvet and lace stripes that run vertically down the front. I'm pairing it with some leather heels from Steve Madden, which will give me a little extra height for a more elegant look.

Well, my loves, that is all you need to know for this New Year's Eve, I hope you have the time of your lives!

You're my everything goals,

Lots of love, Harper

CHAPTER 1

He's Not a Ghost, He Just Plays One on TV

Two years later and my life is nothing like it was. I'm a sophomore in high school, my braces are gone, and then there's the little fact that I've developed a YouTube following of over one million gorgeous fans. My following started off small, just some local girls liking and sharing my videos. Then one day about nine months ago, Kate Hudson tweeted about my YouTube channel, and that's when things took off. And I mean *really* took off. I'm not telling you this so that you think I'm cool (I'm not cool, I swear), just so that you understand why I am where I am when this story begins: a New Year's Eve party hosted by Adam Levine at the Chateau Marmont. No big deal, as they say. This isn't normal for me; I don't hang out at celebrity parties on a day-to-day basis, but I've been invited to this particular event by Mia Vladianova, a high-end fashion designer from Russia who swears that the dishy Maroon 5 lead singer is her ultimate muse. Mia had recently found my channel and taken a liking to it, and much to my surprise, began throwing his swoonworthy clothes at me to wear in my videos.

Hey, I can't complain.

Let me paint the scene:

I'm in a blue velvet jumper with sparkly blue tights, feeling conspicuously younger than everyone else while A-list celebs confidently, casually hover by the bar, laughing and drinking, sometimes posing for a pic, all the while basking in the glow of their comfort zones. I see Kanye brush a crumb off Kim's flawless shoulder, and I couldn't possibly feel more anxious.

"Hey, relax a little, will you?" Ellie says in her diluted Australian accent, grabbing my arm and practically shaking it loose from its socket. Thank God Mia said I could bring Ellie, otherwise there's no way I would have felt brave enough to come to this thing. Ellie Montell is a friend and fellow YouTuber whom I absolutely adore. She's mostly a DIY girl; her videos show step-by-step directions to making any number of things at home by yourself—birdhouse, bird feeder, birdbath, a printed bird tote . . . Yeah, to be honest I think most of her videos are about birds in one way or another. Ever since the day we met, we've had an incredible sisterly bond unlike anything else I've experienced. I still hang out with the Jessicas at school, but it's really not the same. They don't get me or my life the way Ellie gets me. She's new to the world of YouTube, and I have taken her under my wing (pun intended). However, while I have a lot to teach her about building a YouTube following, she has a lot to teach me about socializing and being an overall non-nervous wreck. Ellie can happily strike up a conversation with anyone, and I admire her tremendously for it. You'd think I would be more comfortable with people by now, but if anything, becoming famous by being in front of a camera has made me *more* introverted and insecure.

"I'm trying," I say. "But a normal party is scary enough, let alone one where everyone is famous. Oh my god, is that Nicki Minaj?"

"Where?" She turns to look as Nicki breezes by, platinum blond extensions swishing back and forth. "Oh, yeah, but who cares? They're all just people. And you deserve to be here just as much as anyone else does, okay? Let's get some bubbly. You gotta loosen up a bit, you're starting to scare me."

I wrinkle my nose at her. "Ellie, you know we can't drink."

"I meant Cokes." She shrugs her shoulders up to her strawberry blond bob. "All you need is something to hold while you talk to people, something to sip on if you need a moment to think of what to say or just need a sweet distraction from the social anxiety."

"I thought you *were* my sweet distraction from the social anxiety?"

"Awwww, love ya, girl." She scrunches up her freckled nose. "But no, you need a drink in your hand." She leads me by the elbow up to the bar, where she wriggles us through the crowd of Armani and Versace and assertively orders two Cokes with limes. She even winks at the bartender, who is tan and pretty handsome, but not my type. His hair is too perfectly groomed, gelled back off his forehead in a do so stiff it looks like it could be a helmet. Ew.

We clink our glasses together and I have barely taken my first sip before we're interrupted by a beautiful brunette with glitter eyelash extensions and matching acrylic nails. It's Mooney Blue, pop star extraordinaire. I remember two years ago when her first single came out, "Love at First Listen"—and it had been love at first listen indeed.

"Sorry to interrupt," she says, not seeming that sorry, "but are you Harper Ambrose? You are, aren't you?" Her voice is raspy and smooth at the same time. Effortless and breezy but with a mysterious hint of darkness.

"Um, yeah." I can feel my forehead sweating. "I mean yes. Hi."

"I'm Mooney!" She puts out her hand and I go to shake it, super self-conscious about how shaky my hand feels. "I just wanted to tell you how much I love your videos. Especially the one about what to wear on New Year's! Look!" She steps back so I can see her outfit more clearly: a rose-gold sequined romper with blue leather booties and the same blue glitter tights that I'm wearing.

"Oh my god." I smile, trying not to let on how nervous I am. "You took my advice!"

"I even had my makeup person watch the video so she could know the look I wanted to go with! Honestly, I think you're awesome. It was great meeting you!" She squeezes my hand goodbye and saunters theatrically off into the throng of partygoers.

"That was pretty cool," Ellie says casually while I stare, dumbfounded, at the spot where Mooney was just standing. "Aren't you glad you started making YouTube videos?"

"Yes. Oh my god, Ellie, did I come off as a total space cadet? What's wrong with me?"

"Nothing! You're perfect. You're just a little shy. You can work on it, but in the meantime I think it's endearing."

"That's why you're my best—"

That's when I turn and see the single most gorgeous guy who has ever existed on planet earth. My heart practically pops from my chest cartoon-style. His eyes are bright green and glowing from across the room; his light brown hair is messy and casually swooped to one side; his jaw is so perfect it had to be sculpted by Michelangelo himself; his white-collared shirt is unbuttoned at the neck; and my god, I even love his collarbones. I'm so in awe of this creature that my brain takes a moment to catch up with my eyes before I realize that this isn't just any hot guy, but Dalton James, the British film and TV actor. But mostly film. And sometimes stage. When I was nine, I saw him in a Broadway production of *Oliver Twist,* in which he was riveting and adorable, even back then. Of course he's most famous for the *Sacred* trilogy (ghosts, goblins; a supernatural battle between good and evil; romance naturally ensues . . .), which is what ultimately catapulted him to international stardom. Entranced, I watch him high-five a buddy I don't recognize, then laugh at something I can't hear. The whole thing happens practically in slow motion, at least to my lovesick eyes.

"Helloooo? Harper? *Harper Jessica Ambrose*! I'm your best . . . your best what?" I feel Ellie's acrylic nail extensions pinch my arm and am snapped aggressively back to reality.

"What happened?" I stammer like a recovering coma victim. I might as well have added a *Where am I?*

"You tell me! You completely checked out. I've been trying to get your attention for a good fifteen seconds. Almost had to throw my drink in your face."

I laugh. "Thank you for not doing that."

"You're welcome. So what are you staring at?"

"It's Dalton James. I've had a crush on him for as long as I can remember."

"That pale ghost boy from *Sacred*?"

"He's not so pale in real life. Look." I direct her attention toward Dalton across the patio, where he is now sipping from a Coke can handed to him by anonymous buddy number one.

"Wow," she admits, "that is one smoldering ghost."

"He's not a ghost! He just plays one on TV. Well, in the movies."

"Yes, Harper, I *do* understand that he's not an *actual* ghost." She rolls her eyes at me and we giggle in a way that I haven't done in years. "You gotta go talk to him!"

"I'm sorry, *what*?"

"Go say hi! You'll beat yourself up over it later if you don't."

"I'll beat myself up even more if I go over there and make a fool out of myself!"

"Oh, you won't. You'll be super charming, it will be great."

I roll my eyes at Ellie. "Um, hello, have you *met* me? I will most certainly make a fool out of myself. I'll freeze up and regret the whole thing for the rest of my life."

"Okay, fine, so you'll freeze up or you'll trip or you'll say something horribly embarrassing, but I promise you that will be better than if you never seize the moment and have to live in a constant state of wondering what could have been. I know it sounds cliché, but I'm your friend and you've been saying you want to start living life to the fullest and get over this shyness spell, so I'm gonna make you!" She spoke triumphantly, snatching my uncased rose-gold iPhone 6s out of my hand.

"What are you doing?! Give me my phone, weirdo."

"Nope. Not until you go talk to Dalton."

"Oh my god, you're insane." I try to grab for my phone, but Ellie dances away from me.

"*Am I?*"

"Yes. I'm going to murder you."

"I'm doing you a *huge* favor. Please just try to trust me on this one?"

"Do I have a choice?"

She smirks, still palming my phone. "Not really, no."

"Ugh, Ellie, I hate you." I give her my meanest scowl and turn to go.

"Love ya too, girl!" she calls after me as I walk toward him, all sensation leaving my body.

The space I have to navigate through to get to him is small but crowded. I timidly mutter "Excuse me" and "Pardon me" as I inch my way toward where he's standing, where he's leaning against one of many strategically placed houndstooth armchairs. *Do not use the term "biggest fan,"* I repeat to myself. *Whatever you do, do not use the term "biggest fan."*

"Hey, man, loved you in *Sacred*." A guy in a white T-shirt and red beanie passes by, pointing his fingers in the shape of a gun at Dalton.

"Thanks, man," Dalton responds coolly, and next thing I know I'm standing right there, face-to-face with him. Dalton James. *The* Dalton James.

"You must get that all the time," I say, gripping the glass of Coke tightly with two hands.

"Oh, about *Sacred*? Yeah." He almost blushes. "But it's nice. It's a great project to be a part of. I'm Dalton." He puts out his hand and I shake it hesitantly. That British accent is almost too much to handle.

"I'm Harper."

"Harper," he repeats, smiling, "like someone who plays the harp."

"That's a harpist, actually."

"Right! I knew that."

"Well, nice to meet you." I smile timidly and search for Ellie in the crowd. Yes! I did it! I got through a conversation with Dalton James without looking like a total idiot. If anything, maybe I even came off as kind of cool.

"No, hey, don't go yet, I don't know anything about you!" *Wait, did he just really say that? Am I having a stroke?* I consider pinching myself but don't want to risk ruining the cool-girl vibe I've got going on.

"Me? What do you wanna know?"

"Well, like, what do you do?"

"Oh, I'm a . . . I make YouTube videos." Ugh, I hate how trivial it can sound sometimes. Like, who *doesn't* make YouTube videos? Any moron with a camera phone can do it. Not any moron with a camera phone can get over one million channel subscribers, but I would sound *so* obnoxious if I said that, so I keep that sentiment to myself. It's sort of true, though; I've worked so hard to get where I am, and it frustrates me sometimes that people think it's easy as *one, two, three* to put yourself out there like that, for all of the public to see and judge. And that doesn't even cover the editing, designing, and planning that goes into making the videos look good!

"What kind of YouTube videos?" He crosses his arms, looking as if he might actually be interested in what I have to say. Could this really be happening?

"Mostly makeup and do-it-yourself tutorials. It doesn't sound that exciting, I know, but I'm Harper Ambrose, you can look me up and check out my channel. I mean, if you feel like it."

He pulls out his phone right then and there, types my name into the Google search bar.

"Oh, you don't have to watch those now," I say hurriedly. He's clicking on a Christmas ornament tutorial and my face is burning up—I'm sure I'm turning bright red.

"These are adorable! Well, you're adorable, if you don't mind me saying."

My voice goes breathy and quiet. "I don't mind."

"Hey, listen, I have to go mingle with some people I don't care for all that much, but there's a party at the Magic Castle this coming Friday. Would you . . . would you possibly want to come?"

"Really?" I try not to squeal like a little girl. "I mean, yes, of course. I've always wanted to go there."

"You've never been? Oh, you'll love it, it's spectacular. What's your phone number?"

Head spinning, the blood rushing loud in my ears, I recite my number and he types it quickly into his phone, then types in my name and adds a harp emoji. I have an inside joke with Dalton James?! What is this night turning into? WHAT IS MY LIFE?

I could stand there all night just staring at him dreamily, but then I remember a tip from an old how-to-flirt video I watched once: always leave them wanting more. I assume my best bored face and examine my nails. "All right, I'm gonna go find my friend. She's probably wondering what's taking me so long."

"Wait a minute, did you leave your friend to come talk to me?" he teases.

"Maybe."

"And here I was thinking you barely knew who I was. My feelings were almost hurt, you know."

"Of course I know who you are," I sputter, "I'm your . . . I mean, I'm a—"

"You're . . ."

"I'm *not* your biggest fan," I blurt. "I told myself I wasn't going to say that, so I'm not." Oh god, Harper. Oh my freaking god. For a second I think I might cry, but then he smiles at me.

"You're definitely not my biggest fan, you're too tiny. My biggest fan is probably at *least* three times your size."

"Ha, well, I don't know about—"

Dalton's buddy starts pulling him away toward another section of the party. He turns to catch my eye as he's yanked into the crowd. "I'm looking forward to it, Harper. I'll call you, okay?"

And then he's gone.

"Jesus Christ, Ellie, I can't believe I did that. I cannot believe you made me do that." I'm breathing as heavily as if I had just made it through a SoulCycle class when I get back to Ellie, still in disbelief over what just happened.

"Good or bad, Harper? Good or bad?"

"Good! But also so bad! I totally embarrassed myself, just like I knew I would. I even told him I was his biggest fan, which I promised myself I wouldn't do, but—"

"But what? But what?"

"He asked me out!"

"Like, on a date?"

"Like on a date! I think."

"Oh my god. You're such a rock star. Well, you certainly deserve *this* back." She reaches into her Kitson clutch and hands me back my phone.

"Thank you! Oh, you were so right, Elle—" I freeze when I see my phone screen light up with a text from a 323 area code number that reads:

Pleasure to meet you, Harper. Get excited for the Magic Castle!

"What is it?" Ellie asks.

"He already texted me. *Dalton James* texted me."

"You have Dalton James's number in your phone."

"Eeee!"

"You're going on a date with Dalton James."

"Eeee!"

"Imagine if you hadn't talked to him! Damn, I'm a good friend."

Ellie looks quite pleased with herself, and I don't know if I've ever loved my bestie more than in this moment.

"You are, oh you really are. Ellie, can we get out of here? I think this has been enough excitement for one night. Plus, I don't think I'll be able to stand on these heels much longer without breaking an ankle."

"You got it, babe," she says. "Let's blow this Popsicle stand."

I kick off my heels to drive us home in my purple MINI Cooper convertible. Ellie puts her feet up on the passenger dashboard and crosses her ankles. We blast Katy Perry as we cruise down Sunset, then swerve into In-N-Out for impromptu end-of-night chocolate milk shakes. No matter how incredible a night I've had, no matter what has gone down, it's never complete until I've had a milk shake with my BFF.

This, I think, *is the life.*

TUTORIAL #2

How to Be a Morning Person

1. Tip number one is, Don't hit that snooze button! It's the first thing I want to do when that alarm goes off, but that extra ten minutes of snooze time actually disturbs your sleep cycle and makes you feel more tired.
2. Tip number two is to write down your genius ideas! Or at least the ones you had while you were asleep, just so that you remember them. It helps your brain start to think and wake up.
3. Tip number three is to not worry about yesterday. Today is a new day and you don't have to worry about those M&M's you spent all last night eating. It's okay, guys, you can move on.
4. Tip number four is to think of something to look forward to. For example, I just remembered that *The Bachelor* is on tonight and I got really excited.
5. Something that really wakes me up in the morning is to chug a really cold bottle of water. It's really refreshing and really wakes you up.
6. Open up the blinds straightaway. Letting light into your room helps get your eyes adjusted and ready for the day!
7. My last tip is to get your blood flowing! And you can do this either by working out or having a dance party . . . while making your bed!
8. So once you're all refreshed and awake, it's obviously time to do makeup and hair and get dressed for school, so that is what

I'm doing: same thing I always do, just a simple everyday kind of makeup thing going on. And then I'm putting my hair in a topknot because lazy. Team lazy. Hashtag lazy.

9. Next is the age-old struggle: finding an outfit. I normally just pick up something from the floor from the day before that doesn't smell too bad, and you know, just throw it on. If only it was that easy: just throwing it on, like literally onto yourself.

So, yeah, that's pretty much all you need to know to become a morning person. I hope you liked it, loved it, and learned from it!

You're my everything goals.
Lots of love, Harper

CHAPTER 2

High School Is the First Ring of Hell

Three days later my alarm goes off at six-thirty and I wake up in my baby-blue canopy bed, hating how early it is. As I've done every morning since I met Dalton, I reach for my phone and see his text, then issue a deep sigh of relief: Dalton James. *The* Dalton James. My wildest dreams are coming true. Well, not my *wildest* dreams. My wildest dreams would be that now winter break would never end and high school would be a thing of the past. But alas, the new year has come, and with it the first day back at school.

I like to think of my bedroom as more of a lair, which creates a coolness factor that makes up for the fact that it's in the basement of my parents' house. Being sixteen and Internet famous is hard: I've seen all that's out there waiting for me in this gigantic world, but I'm too young to go out and tackle it on my own. Even so, I'm grateful for all the space my parents give me; letting me convert the basement was undeniably pretty cool of them.

Down in my lair slash hideaway slash sanctuary, I have

everything I could ever need: memory foam mattress with blue satin bedding and canopy, white-painted desk for my computers, floor-to-ceiling bookcase, floor-to-ceiling mirrors, blond hardwood floors, 62-inch flat-screen TV, Audrey Hepburn poster (framed), antique-style wardrobe and vanity (complete with vanity mirror), mini fridge filled with pressed juice and cold-brew coffee, and peach damask curtains for the rectangle of window where the walls meet the ceiling. I like to create my own lighting. Especially when I'm filming a video.

Today's video is "How to Be a Morning Person." This video is just as much for me as it is for my followers, as waking up is a major challenge and constant struggle for me. Hashtag the struggle is real! Hashtag can't stop, won't stop snoozing.

I film about forty minutes of footage that I will have to edit down to about five before posting (editing is half the fun!), then trudge my way upstairs for a yummy breakfast with my parents.

When I get to the top of the basement stairs I come alive with the smell of chocolate chip pancakes.

"Oh my god, Dad, are you serious?" I clap my hands together in delight when I see my dad by the stove, wearing an apron that says *Kiss the Cook* and wielding a spatula.

"Fresh off the skillet, chocolate chip pancakes with a side of sliced bananas." Blue-striped pajamas visible under his apron, he slides a batch of pancakes onto a plate.

"Thank you from the bottom of my heart, father mine. This is exactly what I needed." I bound over to the fridge, grab the OJ and a glass from the cabinet, and scoot over to the kitchen table.

"You're very welcome." He kisses me on the forehead as he sets a steaming stack of pancakes in front of me.

"How was the party last night, honey?" This from my mom, who's walking into the kitchen from the stairs that lead to their bedroom. Her hair is in curlers, and even though it's only seven in the morning and she's still in her favorite terry-cloth robe, she's already wearing her pinkish-brown signature lipstick.

"It was . . . nice. You know"—I take a bite of my pancake—"nothing out of the ordinary."

"Oh, really? Then why are you blushing?" She eyes me suspiciously as she pours herself a cup of coffee.

"I'm not!"

"Did you meet a *boyyyy*?" she teases in a singsong voice.

"So, Dad, great pancakes." I change the subject. "Did you use extra chocolate chips? Tastes amazing."

"Same chocolate chips as always," he says proudly. "But I added a slug of vanilla extract."

"Fascinating." I chew. "And no more out of you, missy!" I say jokingly, cutting my mom off as she's gearing up for more interrogating.

"Fine." She gives up. "Honestly I'm just glad you're up early enough for school. And you finished up your homework before you went out last night, right?"

"That's because you guys won't let me let parties and boys get in the way of my education," I point out, using my fork for emphasis. "And yes. I finished my homework."

"You know the rule, get your high school diploma and the rest is up to you," Dad chimes in. "Whatever you want. Shave your head, join the circus, see if we care."

"Ew, no. I have big plans for my YouTube career, and I would *never* get more than a trim, let alone shave my head—you know that." I run my hands over my most prized possession: my long, wavy brown hair that reaches down below my rib cage. When I was a little girl I dreamed of having Rapunzel-length hair, and TBQH (to be QUITE honest), I've gotten pretty darn close, thanks to my iron will and John Frieda.

My mom looks pointedly at the clock on the wall. "Speaking of school, Harper . . ."

I groan and shovel the last of the pancakes into my mouth. "What? I have time."

"Barely, honey. Maybe if you spent less time on those videos, you'd have time to eat a full breakfast. I know, I *know*, such a mom thing to say, but I had to say it."

"My videos are important! I need them to live." Every now and then I have to throw them a little typical teenage melodrama for the sake of giving them the real, full parenting experience.

"Funny," Dad quips, "I heard you needed breakfast to live, but what do I know?"

"Ha-ha. Good one, Dad. Fine. Bye, guys. See you later, gators."

I hug my parents goodbye, throw my books into my backpack and my backpack over my shoulder, and am out the door.

Oh, high school, how I hate you with the passion and heat of a million suns! Last semester we read Dante's *Inferno* and all I could think was *High school is the first ring of hell*. What do I hate about high school? Oh, pretty much just about everything. Where do I begin? The girls are mean and the boys are just dumb, the teachers are mostly bitter, and the administration is over-the-top uptight. Walking through the front gates of the school, I feel as though it was a lifetime ago, not a measly three days, that I was rubbing elbows with celebs and talking to Dalton James. Ellie has the unique luxury of being homeschooled, so she doesn't have to endure this type of torture. Lucky brat.

I'm sitting in Mr. Gomez's third-period algebra class feeling restless and distracted by the sun shining oh so brightly just outside the window. Mr. Gomez has long hair that he ties back into a ponytail, and his eyes are always suspiciously bloodshot. One time he made the mistake of showing us how he can do a push-up on only three fingers, and now barely ten minutes go by without some kid asking to see it again. He's actually a pretty cool guy and maybe one of my favorite teachers, even though I don't care for math. He makes everything a lot easier to understand. Plus, he grades homework by writing down a number from one to four based on how much you've accomplished, and it's really easy to change a one into a four. Not that I'm encouraging cheating in school. I'm just saying we all have our different strengths and weaknesses, and life is about figuring out what works for you and then celebrating it.

Anyway, I'm sitting in Mr. Gomez's algebra class feeling restless and distracted by the beautiful day outdoors. Mr. Gomez is pointing to the quadratic formula written on the whiteboard, breaking it down for us piece by tedious piece, but he might as well be preaching the imminent arrival of doomsday, because I CANNOT

FOCUS. All I can think of is Dalton and the way he kept looking at me last night. I have to resist the urge to dig through my bag for my phone and read his text message for the millionth time. What does a big shot like Dalton James want with a mere plebeian like myself?

Sigh. If only I could break free from the oppressive cage that is high school: I'd run to Dalton's place, probably some gorgeous mansion in the Hollywood Hills, and we'd fly off to England in his probably private jet, where he'd introduce me to his probably amaze parents, and meet the probably even more amaze queen, and—

Wait. What was that?

I feel a bit of pressure on the back of my head and quickly grope for it with my hands. It's a piece of gum. Chewed gum. In my hair. I whip around to see Ashley Adler smirking at me with her stupid evil eyes and her blindingly shimmery blond bob. Ugh.

Oh, Ashley Adler, what a piece of work. What a mean, spoiled, insecure, petty girl. See, ever since the first day of high school, Ashley Adler had been the most popular girl in our grade, the queen bee, if you will. She ignored me 100 percent, but I noticed how she'd pick on other girls; anyone she thought was weird or different posed a threat to her sense of self, so she'd try to tear them down. Why people worshiped her, I had no idea. I guess it was the royal treatment you'd get if you were on her good side, the parties you'd be invited to and the elite status you'd receive. Then I blew up on YouTube and that put me on her radar. It put me right smack in the middle of her radar, actually. Suddenly kids at school wanted to talk to me, they wanted to be my friend, they wanted me to like them, and Ashley hated it. Attention on me took attention off her, so she often went out of her way to undermine me in an attempt to take back her throne. The thing was, I didn't even want the throne, I wished she'd just take it and leave me alone.

"I'm sorry, but did you just put gum in my hair?" I try to stay calm and collected as I whisper at her, desperate not to attract attention but on the verge of tears. I try to tell myself it won't be that bad, but in my mind I'm imagining the very worst.

She shrugs. "Oops, must've slipped out. Sorry." But she's not sorry. Her group of Brandy Melville model wannabe friends snicker in the back row.

I grit my teeth. "I swear to God, Ashley—"

"Ladies, is there something wrong back there?"

Ashley looks up at our teacher and smiles sweetly. "No, Mr. Gomez, we're all chill. Right, Harper?"

"No, wrong, Ashley." I can't hold back or be chill, not when my hair is involved. "You put gum in my hair. Who does that? Are you in kindergarten?" And in spite of my biggest efforts I'm on the verge of tears.

Ashley rolls her eyes at me. "Whoa, way to be a snitch, Internet girl."

"All right, all right." Mr. Gomez walks over tentatively and helplessly chimes in (even the teachers are intimidated by Ashley), "Ashley, can you try to be less of a bully? It's getting a little tiring. And Harper, it's just gum, so let's try to calm down."

"It's JUST gum?! Do you not know what gum does to hair? It's like . . . it's like . . . the nuclear war of hair."

"Drama queen," Ashley mutters.

"You know what? I don't need this." And I really don't. I sling my backpack over my shoulder and hurry out of the class.

"Harper!" Mr. Gomez calls after me. "You can't just—oh, forget it, I'm getting too old for this shit," I hear him say as the classroom door swings shut behind me.

I'm racing down the hallway toward the bathrooms with my hand cupped around the gum to prevent further humiliation when all of a sudden SMACK! I collide head on with none other than Jack Walsh. Yeah, him—Mister Dream Boy from a few years and some pages ago.

"Oh god." I stumble backward and am about to fall, but he catches me. I shake him off me and back away, one hand still gripping the hunk of gum-infused hair. "I'm good, I got it. Thanks."

"What's up with you?" he asks, concerned and slightly amused. "You look kinda . . . flustered." Three years have changed Jack, and not necessarily for the better. For starters, his vision went south and he had to get glasses, which make some guys cuter, but not him—his eyes look far away and kind of beady. Second of all, he still wears baggy skater-boy pants and puts too much gel in his hair—I mean, Dalton would never be caught dead looking like that. Third of all, for some completely mysterious reason, the smooth-guy charisma and charm he had in middle school has vanished almost entirely. Instead he's withdrawn and almost antisocial. Except with me. When it comes to me, for the past year, he's been suspiciously . . . interested.

"I'm fine," I grind out. "Ashley Adler put gum in my hair. I'm just going to the bathroom to, you know, try to get it out or whatever."

"Oh, damn, I'm sorry, Harper."

"You'd think being Internet famous would make me likable in school, not a walking target for bullies. It's completely counterintuitive." This has been a frustrating reality for some time now.

"It's because they're jealous. They see you succeeding at something you love, and they know they'll never amount to anything."

"Thanks. But I think maybe they're just brats."

"I remember when my little sister would get gum stuck in her hair and my mom would have to cut it out and then her hair would be super uneven and awkward, so then she'd have to go to the Yellow Balloon to get a really short—I'm sorry, this isn't helping."

"No. No, it's not." I try to shoulder past him. "Excuse me, I gotta take care of this."

"Let me help you. I know some good tricks from back when this used to happen to Marnie."

"Your sister with the lopsided haircuts? No thanks."

"Harper, I'm just trying to be nice."

"Great, but I don't need nice right now. I need for you to get out of my way so that I can get this gum out of my hair before it really sets and I have to get a freaking pixie cut, okay?"

He looks so disappointed as I hurry away that for a moment I almost feel bad for him.

It might seem like I'm being harsh on Jack, but honestly all I'm doing is protecting myself. I was in love with this guy for all of middle school. I would have walked a tightrope between two skyscrapers for the chance to be his girlfriend, but guess what? He didn't want that. And why didn't he want that? Because I was dorky and clumsy; I had glasses and braces and bad skin and didn't know how to handle my rapidly growing limbs, which often caused me to walk around looking like a drunken marionette. Even after Gwen disappeared and they broke up—it was all anyone could talk about at school for days—he never wanted me, even though I couldn't have made myself more available. But now that my glasses and braces are gone and my skin has cleared up and I have boobs and a million YouTube subscribers . . . well, NOW he's interested. I may not be old and wise, but I'm no dummy: I know I deserve better than a guy who likes me only for my looks or my fame.

The mirrors in the girls' bathroom look like they're fogged up, but it's actually just really, really old glass. With my matte lilac coffin-shaped acrylics I pick my precious strands of hair one by one out of the disgusting glob of bubble gum until all but a few stubborn pieces are still stuck. Goddammit. I remember once reading that peanut butter helps get gum out of hair, and thank goodness I just happen to have a peanut butter and jelly sandwich in my lunch. Now, they don't say anything about putting jelly in your hair, but a girl's gotta do what a girl's gotta do. Before I know it, I have gobs of peanut butter and jelly all over my head and I'm no closer to getting the gum out. Now what?! In panic mode, I turn on the sink and bend over backward so that the water washes through my hair.

"Please come out," I say out loud. "Please, please, let my hair be okay."

I stand back up and reach for the gum spot, massage my fingers through the hair around it, trying to loosen the knot. Nothing. The gum won't move. The gum won't move and now I have peanut butter and jelly and water running down my brand-new Theory shirt. I have no choice, I have to do the unthinkable: I take a pair of scissors out of my backpack and carefully snip through here and there, removing the gum in its entirety like a surgeon. However, just as I suspected, I am ultimately unable to save my hair from permanent damage: there is now a section of short, defiant flyaways that will take forever to grow back. Well, isn't this day shaping up to be just peachy?

At lunch, I find the Jessicas where they always sit: in a tight circle under the biggest oak tree on the front lawn. Ever since I met Ellie, my friendship with the Jessicas has started to seem somewhat . . . lackluster. Don't get me wrong, they're cool girls and great lunchtime companions, but I just don't click with them the way I do with Ellie. They only ever want to talk about high-school-related gossip and what colleges they want to go to and fad diets that they want to try or are afraid to try or are currently trying (there's lots of trying involved, obviously). In the year and a half that I've known them, I've never really gotten to a place where I feel I can be myself around them. And now that I have mega followers, they've started walking on eggshells around me, always trying (here we go again) to say the right thing, as if my small amount of fame has made me into a different person. Or maybe it's that they think my videos are lame and they've lost all respect for me. Who knows? Either way, hanging with the Jessicas has lost its charm.

Today when I approach them, they treat me extra delicately.

"Harper!" Jessie jumps to her feet when she sees me. "Are you okay? We heard what Asshole Adler did to your poor hair!" One awesome thing about the Jessicas is that they hate Ashley and her posse even more than I do. Before I met them in high school, they all went to middle school together. Apparently Ashley spread rumors that they stuffed their bras, and made a habit out of telling the boys they liked that they were lesbians.

"I'm fine, I'm fine. I just have this gnarly patch of botched hair now. Bu it's a small patch. And hair grows back, right? So no biggie." I take a deep breath and sit down, and then Jessie follows my lead.

"You're so brave!" Jessa says, stroking my arm. "I can't believe she did that to you."

"So immature," agrees Jess.

"Well, joke's on her because now I have a great excuse to skip the rest of the day and go shopping."

"You can't skip. We have SAT prep fifth period," Jess reminds me.

"Dammit. I completely forgot." I think it through for a moment. "I'll probably just skip it anyway."

"But you skipped last week."

"So?"

"So you need a lot of practice if you want to get a good score."

"But I don't even know if I'm going to take the SATs. It seems sort of unnecessary to practice for something I'm not going to do."

"Harper, if you don't take the SATs you will never get into college."

"But I don't want to go to college!"

"You don't?" Jess stares as if I've just told her I'm visiting from Mars.

"No, I want to have time to work on my videos and focus on developing my career. See how far I can take this whole YouTube thing."

"You're so lucky." Jessie sighs.

"I'm not lucky. Any one of you could do it too."

"Oh, I couldn't," Jessa says. "My parents would kill me if I didn't go to college."

"And besides," adds Jessie, "not just anyone can become a YouTube star. You have to have the right personality and the determination. You gotta have star power. You have that, Harper, we don't."

I have to laugh. "Me? Star power? You're definitely wrong." How anyone could see me as anything other than a clumsy, unhip mess is beyond me. I suppose Internet fame has helped me develop a certain amount of likability, but star power? I never thought I'd hear myself be described with those words.

"We're not wrong," Jessa says. "It's your star quality that makes people want to watch you. One million people! You can't deny it. If you didn't have star quality, you wouldn't have followers, trust me."

"Maybe," I say, not because I agree but because all this attention is making me uncomfortable and I want to change the subject.

Jessie practically swoons. "I think it's great you don't want to take the SATs. You walk to the beat of your own drum and you don't let other people tell you how to live your life."

"Jessie," Jess scolds her, "stop enabling her. Harper"—she turns to face me—"they're right, you're special and successful and beautiful, but you're also really smart, and as your friend I can't let you turn away so easily from the possibility of getting an education. The truth is, you don't know what you really want yet. You don't know what's best for you. None of us do. That's why we have to go through the motions of life until we figure it out. Not to mention college could really help you grow your brand. How else are you going to get educated in marketing and business? As your friend, I really think you should come with us to SAT prep today."

"Or what?" I ask.

"Or I'll cry! You don't want me to cry, do you?"

I didn't want her to cry. I mean, I didn't believe she actually would, but I didn't feel like taking a chance. Plus, I liked that Jess had dropped the kiss-Harper's-butt act to do what she thought was best for me. It meant she was a real friend.

That's how I've come to be sitting in fifth-period SAT prep, taught by none other than Coach Flanders, head of the boys' water polo team. I regretted my decision as soon as I sat in my seat. The classroom is in the basement of the language building, so there is no source of natural light and no fresh air to breathe. There are chalkboards on every wall, so not only is the squeaky sound of chalk a constant, but also the air is always thick with chalk dust.

"How kind of you to join us this week, Miss Ambrose," Coach Flanders teases as I take a seat behind the Jessicas. "Decided there might be more important things than YouTube, did we?"

There are two types of teachers, in my opinion: the type that get into teaching because they find pleasure in educating and making a difference in a child's life, and the type that failed at everything else until the only option left was teaching. It's not hard to spot which is which. Coach Flanders is the latter. He resents his students, and more than that, he resents success.

"Sure," I say, not wanting to give him any more ammo than he already has.

"Okeydokey." He grabs a stack of test booklets and starts handing them out. "You're here for the next two and a half hours whether you like it or not, so you might as well accept it. We'll start as we always do, with a quick practice run. Then we'll score our tests and go over the right answers so we can see where we went wrong." If you ask me, the booklets are more like full-on books, thick and daunting. I can't see how this could possibly be a "quick" practice run. He sets the timer and I open my "booklet" to the first page. Math. Great. So that you can understand my dread in the moment, here is what the page looks like:

1. If $2x + 2x + 2x + 2x = 2(16)$, what is the value of x?
2. The lengths of two sides of a triangle are 3 and 8. What is the greatest possible integer length of the third side?
3. The coordinates (x,y) of each point on the circle above satisfy the equation $a^2 + a^2 = 50$. Line M is tangent to the circle at

point C. If the x-coordinate of point C is 3, what is the slope of M?

Oh, boy. Math has never been my thing; my brain just doesn't work that way. So naturally I can feel the beginnings of a small panic attack rolling in on the horizon. It's okay, I try to tell myself, you're only here so Jess doesn't cry. It doesn't matter if you don't know the answers. But I can't help but feel a pang of shame, as if not knowing (or caring) how to solve these problems is a reflection on my incompetence as a human being. I flip away from the math section and to the vocabulary. I figure this should make me feel better about myself, and it does. I know the definitions of practically all the words:

1. Abhor: *hate*
2. Counterfeit: *fake*
3. Noxious: *poisonous*
4. Placid: *calm, peaceful*
5. Talisman: *lucky charm*
6. Abrasive: *rough, coarse, harsh*
7. Replete: *full*
8. Tangible: *can be touched*

I fly through this section, wishing there was such a thing as the vocabulary-only SATs. I close the booklet and close my eyes. Finally I have a moment to myself to breathe and dip back into the memories of last night: Dalton's hand on my shoulder, Dalton's classic British accent with that perfect amount of bad-boy flare . . .

To distract myself from the events of the day (the Great Hair Disaster and the Math Catastrophe), I take out my phone (careful to hide it beneath my test 'booklet') and type Dalton James into the search bar. *Don't be a fangirl*, I tell myself, *don't be a fangirl*. But I can't help it. I hit search and there's no turning back. I start by diving into his Wikipedia page and casually scrolling through. *Dalton Edwin Robert James (born 13 June 1997) is an English actor and model*. Yep, knew that. *James started his career in theater at age seven when he played the titular role in* Oliver Twist *at the Queen's Theatre in London*. Yep, knew that. *He then moved to America and had several small roles on various sitcoms, including* Kelly Life *and* Newton's Laws. Yep, knew that. *In 2012 he got his big break when signing on to play Bobby Malone in Regina Clark's* Sacred *Trilogy*. Yep, knew that. All of this info is pretty basic and getting kind of dull, so I go back to Google and click on a TMZ link that reads: *Trouble for Dalton James?* The article goes like this:

Pop star Jade Taylor admitted yesterday that her latest album, Player Hater, *is all about actor ex-boyfriend Dalton James, who she says cheated on her countless times throughout the relationship. This isn't the first time James has been accused of bad-boy behavior. In 2014, his* Sacred *costar and ex-girlfriend Christina Rush claimed she dumped him after he wouldn't stop partying with fangirls.*

WHAT? Did NOT know that. I can practically feel the steam fuming from my ears. Great, I love finding out that the mega hot celebrity I have a date with might just be pursuing me for sport—for the sake of the hunt. Wonderful.

You know what? I think to myself, clicking off my phone. *I have completely had it with this day*. There's no way I'm staying for sixth period. I watch the minute hand of the clock tick by so slowly it could be moving through molasses, go through the motions of marking up my booklet while Coach Flanders gives us the answers, and as soon as the bell rings, I'm out of there faster than you can say Lemony Snicket.

Everybody hustles to sixth period—that is, everybody but me. Not wanting to attract attention by walking directly away from school, I sneak around to the back of the language building where there's an unguarded fence just low enough for me to climb over. My Jeffrey Campbell platform heels get momentarily stuck in the chain links a few times, and the pleats of my skirt get caught on the spokes, but finally I hop down and am standing on the other side, the side of FREEDOM.

I hop in my MINI Cooper parked on Fourth Street and put the top down, then drive to one of my favorite places, one of the few places on planet Earth where my problems all simply fade away: the Santa Monica Mall.

First things first: I head to Urban Outfitters and pick out a series of adorable and strategic hair accessories to hide the Unfortunate Awkward Spot that is now going to stick with me for the next few months, thanks to Ashley Adler. When life hands me lemons (as it did today), I like to try my best to make lemonade. In other words, if I'm going to be dealing with this chop job (sadly, not something even the most skilled hair stylist could fix), I might as well make the best of it by dressing it up with ribbons, bows, and berets. By the time I'm finished, I have a bag stuffed full of velvet and satin, plaids and stripes, neons and pastels. The lady at the cash register, who herself has at least four facial piercings, probably thinks I'm a psychopath with a basement full of a creepy collection of dolls I like to dress up and talk to and host tea parties with as if they're my friends. Yikes, my mind can really go to some dark places when I let it.

I make my way out of Urban Outfitters, and I find myself staring at the fountain shaped like a Triceratops. It's made out of wire covered with ivy, and water shoots out of its mouth into a pool where people have been throwing pennies since the early nineties. It's like a loose-change graveyard in there. I take my dark-minded self to Wetzel's and buy a cinnamon pretzel before perching on the edge of the Triceratops fountain to chow down, watching pigeons fight over pieces of other people's abandoned snacks. It may seem kind of bleak, but I'd take this over the last three hours of school any day.

Next stop: Brandy Melville. I legitimately love their clothes—literally everything in there is beyond super adorbs—but what is with this whole "one size fits all" thing? How is this tiny gray cotton halter top supposed to fit me AND some girl with gigantic boobs? Or what about some girl who's barely five feet tall? How are she and I supposed to fit into the same size jeans? IT DOESN'T MAKE ANY SENSE. It's like some major Mary Poppins or Sisterhood of the Traveling Pants sorcery.

I'm in the dressing room trying on a bunch of stretchy fabric turtleneck crop tops, and Brandy Melville is playing a bunch of vintage rock songs from the seventies and eighties that I'm kind of getting into, when all of a sudden my phone vibrates and it's A TEXT FROM DALTON.

Thinking about you. Can't stop watching your videos, pretty girl!

Uh-oh, I'm a gonner. Hashtag sa-wooooooooooon. Hashtag heart eyes emoji.

CHAPTER 3

LOL ;)

I have my nose pressed up against the living room window as Ellie drives up in her seafoam green Fiat, and by the time she parks and gets out of her car, I can't possibly pull her into my house fast enough.

"Whoa, whoa, what in the world is going on? Calm down, bb, you're gonna leave bruises on my arm."

"Sorry." I shut the front door behind her and loosen my grip on her arm slightly as I lead her down the basement stairs to my lair. "But we have serious things to discuss."

"Oookay." She sits on the corner of my bed and eyes me like I'm an animal and might be rabid. "Like . . . ?"

"First of all, you know Evil Ashley?"

"How could I forget?"

"Well, today during math class she put gum in my hair, and now look!" I unclip a blue bow from my hair and point dramatically to the dreaded spot.

Ellie's eyes widen in shock. "Oh, Harper, that's . . . I'm so sorry."

"Thank you." I throw my arms around her neck. "Finally somebody understands what I'm going through."

"Cute bow, though."

"Thanks, yeah. It's from Urban."

"Dope." Ellie flops down on my bed. "So what's the second thing we have to talk about? Or was there more to the whole gum-in-hair story?"

"No, that was it."

"Okay, so next item."

"Next item: this text from Dalton." I pull out my phone, open to said text, and hand it to her. "Read, please."

"Wow," she says, her eyes widening in disbelief, "this is incredible. I mean, it's Dalton James. He's . . . well, hot."

"I know."

"So what are you gonna write back?"

"Well, here's the thing. The catch, if you will."

"I'm on the edge of my seat. Literally."

"So I looked him up on Google."

"Naturally."

"And according to Wikipedia, he's dated both Christina Rush and Jade Taylor. And both of them publicly said he was a major player."

"And?"

"That's it."

"Well, duh, you didn't know this? Christina Rush is the main girl in *Sacred*. Everyone knew they were dating—it was a thing.

And Jade Taylor practically wrote a whole album about her relationship with him. He totally broke her heart when he was photographed making out with some random girl in Las Vegas."

"No!" I gasp.

"Are you serious? Have you been living under a rock?"

"On the contrary! I've spent over 75 percent of my life for the past four years on the Internet. How could I have possibly missed this?"

"I don't know. But hey, it's a *good* thing that you don't pay attention to gossip. It's all hearsay anyway. Who knows what's really true?"

"Okay, okay, maybe you're right. So you think I should still text him back?"

"Girl, it's Dalton James. If you don't text him back, I'll do it for you."

"I shouldn't let it bug me that he might have sort of a reputation as a heartbreaker or whatever?"

Ellie shakes her head vehemently. "No, who cares? You don't need to marry the guy, just go on a date, have a fling, you know, for the story or whatever. It's an awesome story to have under your belt. YOLO, right?"

"YOLO." I nod firmly, decision made, and plop down next to Ellie. "Yes. Okay, so what should I say?"

"Oh, this part I'm not good at."

"Well, me neither! Do I say thank you? Do I compliment him back? Do I tell him to stop watching my videos and use his time for something more worthwhile?"

"First of all, you need to pick your self-esteem up off the floor and put it on a pedestal where it belongs."

I laugh. "You're right. He can watch my videos all day if he wants—they're awesome."

"That's the spirit."

"Okay, so what do I say?"

"How about just . . . LOL?"

"*LOL?* LOL what?"

"That's it, just LOL."

"Are you serious? I can't just write LOL!"

"Well, why not?"

"I don't know . . . it's just not . . . it's not a substantial text! He'll think I'm not interested in him."

"Maybe. Or maybe he'll just think you're cool and mysterious."

"Interesting." I think this through. She might have a point. "But it can't be an LOL all by itself. It needs a little something extra."

"Like an emoji?"

"Yes! Perfect. Okay." I take back my phone from her and type LOL, then open up the emoji keyboard. "Wide smile? No, too enthusiastic. Kissy-face? No, too easy. Tongue out? No, *way* too easy. Heart eyes? No—"

"How about a winky face?"

"Hm. What message does a winky face send?"

"It says, *I get you*. It says, *Who knows what's to come?*"

"Really? It says all that?"

"Trust me."

"All right then," I say somewhat skeptically, typing the winky face in next to the LOL. I take a deep breath and hit send.

Ellie squeals. "Oooh, I'm so nervous for you!"

"What do you mean?"

"Well, like, who knows what he's going to write back to that?"

"You said it was a good idea!" I start freaking out a little. "Was it a stupid thing to send? Did we just totally mess this up?!"

Bliinnngggggggg! The phone dings almost immediately. My heart skips a beat. This is the moment of truth.

DALTON JAMES

Where shall I pick you up for our date?

And do you think you can be ready by 8:30?

I flip the phone around to show Ellie and we go wild.

"What did I tell ya, babe?" She grins. "When in doubt, just hit 'em up with an LOL winky."

"I never should have doubted you." I bounce up from the bed and rush to my walk-in closet, flinging the doors open with a flourish. "Eeeeks, I gotta figure out what to wear."

"Do you, though? The date isn't until Friday."

"If I leave the planning 'til Friday I'll end up trying on seventeen hundred dresses in a row and then end up just showing up in whatever pair of jeans happen to be lying on my floor. You know how I get what I leave things to the last minute."

Ellie rolls her eyes. "You *always* leave things to the last minute."

"And I'm trying to change! Starting now. Come on, help me plan."

Just then my phone dings again, only this time it's a different sound, the *whir-whoooosh* sound that means I have a new Twitter notification. Because I have so many followers, getting a notification of any kind is no big shocker, so when I reach for my phone and open Twitter I'm not expecting anything out of the ordinary and am therefore entirely unprepared for the words that appear on my screen:

> **@ThatBitchHarper:** Rumor has it @Harper_Ambrose has a date w/ @DaltonJamesOfficial this Friday. Honey, he is WAY out of ur league. Dalton = Hot. Harper = Not.

Wait, *what*? My heart stops a little. Let me explain: I'm not like some big baby who can't handle the haters. The first rule of fame (Internet or otherwise) is that for every fan you have, you get two haters. Okay, so maybe there's no such rule officially, but it's something I've observed. I can handle the haters because I get them all the time: insecure girls telling me I'm too pale, sad old men in their mom's basements calling me fat or stupid for no apparent reason whatsoever. But this is different. This is a tweet about details of my life that nobody could possibly know. Except for Ellie. And of course Dalton.

"What's wrong?" Ellie asks, pausing halfway to my closet.

"Something weird on Twitter." I try to understand. Who else could possibly know about my date on Friday?

"Let me see. You're kind of freaking me out." I guess my face must have looked as ghostly as it felt. I show her the tweet and she reads it out loud and then laughs a little.

"That's ridiculous. *Dalton equals hot, Harper equals not*? Who is this person and why does he think we're still in the nineties?"

I shake my head slowly. "I have no idea who it could be."

"Does it matter? I mean, who cares? You've gotten way worse than *Harper equals not*. Remember that one time—"

"No, you don't understand. Whoever this is knows about my date with Dalton, and literally the only people who know about it are him and you."

"Whoa." Ellie takes this in. "I didn't think of it like that."

"It can't be you, because you've been sitting here with me this whole time. And it can't be Dalton because . . . why would he do that? Doesn't make sense."

"And you didn't tell anyone else that you're forgetting about?"

"No! I've barely even spoken to anyone since I met him."

Ellie shrugged. "If this is bugging you, we can figure it out. You know I'm here for you. We'll get down to the bottom of this."

"I'll deal with it later," I shake it off, mentally and physically. Ellie's right: I've faced down much, much worse and come out the other side. So what if it's wigging me out a bit that someone out there in the Twittosphere seems to know something private about my life? The fact is, I've got a date with *the* Dalton James Friday night, and whoever that Internet saddo is doesn't. I flash a smile at Ellie and head back to my closet. "Moving on. I've got an outfit to pick out."

TUTORIAL #3

Tumblr Date Ideas

Hi, everyone! This video is gonna be all about date ideas, but, like, honestly you can do these things with your girlfriends too, you don't have to have a BAE. Okay? Okay.

So, what is a Tumblr date? Is it a date that takes place virtually, through Tumblr? Is it a date between two people who met on Tumblr? Neither! It is simply an idea for a date that I got off of Tumblr. Simple. As. That.

1. Tumblr date idea numero uno is to bake something! How many times have you been watching like a cute TV show or movie and the boyfriend and girlfriend are baking something together and they get in a cute food fight and throw things and it just ends up being totes adorbs? If you're trying to flirt with someone, I'm just saying it is the perfect opportunity. I think this one is super good for a first-date idea if you're not really serious yet and just starting off. You can have fun with it, put frosting on their face, burn the cookies, forget the sprinkles, and the whole thing ends up being a total fail, but you just go out for dessert after and it's the perfect little scenario. *Sigh*
2. Tumblr date idea number two is build a fort. I mean, obviously. That is the number one thing you see on Tumblr when you're scrolling through your feed. If you are trying to make out with

someone or kiss someone, a fort is the perfect opportunity. You don't just build a fort with a boy and not kiss him. Doesn't happen. If you build a fort with him and you don't kiss him in that fort, then . . . girl, I can't help ya.

3. Tumblr date idea number three is mini golfing. Eeeee, so cute. Classic. It's a classic. I went to the golf course last week and there was this cute—no, THE CUTEST—Tumblr couple, and I was like why don't I just film them? They totally saw me creeping on them. I mean, who knows? They're probably watching this video right now. I would not be surprised. Hi! It's so good for a first date, or even if you've been dating for a while, to go play games (literal, not figurative—duh).
4. PHOTO BOOTH! OMG. Photo booth. Another great place for if you're trying to kiss someone. Just be like *pose* *pose*, then sneak in for a kiss. Works every time.
5. The last date idea that I came up with for you guys is to have a beach picnic day. If you don't have a beach near where you live, that's totally fine. A lake will do, a pond, a puddle. Okay maybe not a puddle—that might be a little weird. But literally you can just go to a park and have a nice picnic and bring cute little chocolate-covered strawberries (or you can bake something before you go to the park—see idea #1). Am I right? They're the best things ever. Maybe not so good for a first date because they're really romantic—maybe like a fifth or sixth date kind of thing.

Those are some of the date ideas I came up with, but there are honestly so many more. Hiking, rowboating, or canoeing? Yeah, that's really cute. You can be a tourist in your own city! Go to a coffee shop, go on a spontaneous adventure, go to the airport and literally just watch planes take off into the sky. Might seem kind of basic, but it's actually very romantic. Trust me.

You're my everything goals.

Lots of love, Harper

• •

CHAPTER 4

A Number Between One and Five

The last bell on Friday can't come soon enough, and when it does, I bolt out of Mrs. Steinmetz's sixth-period biology faster than you can say "dissected frog." Which might not be that fast, actually, now that I think about it.

By the time I get home it is 3:45, which means I have four hours and fifteen minutes until I have to leave my house to meet Dalton at the Magic Castle. He tried to insist on picking me up, but I refused. If I let him pick me up he would see that I live with my parents, and I just can't have that—he is Dalton James, after all. On the other hand, maybe he already assumes I live with my parents. I mean, what kind of sixteen-year-old *doesn't* live with her parents? Or wait, does he know that I'm sixteen? How old is *he*? For a moment I panic, thinking this romance is already doomed before it begins, but when I refer back to his Wikipedia page, I'm reminded that he was born in 1999, which makes him seventeen, only one year older than I am. For all I know, *he* still lives with *his* parents. You never know.

Anyway, I've got four hours and fifteen minutes to get ready, which means I must start literally *now*.

First I take a bath. This is how I unwind and get rid of butterflies and nerves. The tub in my private basement lair is not that big, nor does it have an exciting view (it *is* in a basement), but I have lined about four million candles up along the porcelain rim for ultimate relaxation. I rest my iPhone on the sink and have it play Enya's album *Shepherd Moons*. When I was a baby, this was the album my mom played to get me to sleep, so my mind is basically programmed to find it soothing. I shave my legs and scrub myself down with a salt and coconut exfoliant, then rest my head against the tile and could easily just fall asleep—but I can't, of course; I have very important things to do!

Once scrubbed and shampooed and conditioned, I dry myself off, slip into a bubblegum-pink fleece robe, and tackle the first grooming task: hair. I blow it dry and then choose a cone curler with a large barrel to create loose, casual easy-breezy curls that say, *Hey, I'm fun and fancy! But mostly fun*. It's that classically effortless look that actually requires quite a bit of effort. In the good old days, that would be it for hair, but now because of this stupid gum fiasco I have to make sure to cover up the awkward spot. I choose to create two braids that cross behind my head, strategically passing over the dreaded choppy area, before lacing a ribbon through it for some extra flare.

I'm in the middle of choosing a ribbon color when there's a knock on my door.

"It's Mom. Can I come in?"

"Of course!" I call up. "It should be open."

Mom comes down into my lair with a cup of hot tea. “I made tea, thought you might like some.”

“Mmm, yes! Thanks, Mom. You da best.”

“Where are you headed, honey? Somewhere fancy?”

“Yes, actually,” I say, choosing a muted coral ribbon. “I’m going on a date at the Magic Castle.”

“Ooh la la! A date with whom, may I ask?”

“Okay, fine, you were right. Remember the other night when you asked if I met a boy and I changed the subject? His name is Dalton and he’s . . . well, he’s Dalton James, the actor.”

“The *movie star*?” Her mouth drops open. She sits on my bed as if suddenly unable to stand on her own two feet.

“Uh-huh.”

“*You* have a date with a *movie star*. I can’t believe this. I mean, I can believe this, I always thought you’d end up with someone famous, I just can’t believe I was right.”

“No one said anything about me ending up with him. It’s just one date. Let’s not get ahead of ourselves.”

“Well? So? Are you excited?”

“Sure, kind of . . . but I’m almost too nervous to be excited.”

“Why, honey?”

“Well, it’s my first date, and—”

“Your first date *ever*? Didn’t you go on a date with Jack?”

“No. That was the whole point of the Jack Fiasco. He didn’t want to date me.”

“Oh my god, I can’t believe my baby is going on her first date! I have to get your father in here!”

"Please don't." I panic for a second, thinking she might actually call my dad in to join us and then we'd have to have one of those awkward talks I've been dreading. And besides, when I'm feeling jittery, the last thing I need is more attention on me.

"Why not? He's your dad. He'll want to see you off on your first date! When will Dalton be here to pick you up?"

"He's not, I'm meeting him there, and it's really not a big deal. Forget I used the word 'date.' Think of this more as a casual meet-up."

"Why are you trying to play this down? It's exciting!"

"I dunno." I lace the ribbon into a braid. "I guess just, like . . . well, you know, he's this super famous actor and I'm just kind of . . . well, *you* know."

"I *don't* know, actually." She laughed. "Sure, you're not a movie star, but—"

"I'm a YouTube star! That's like the least bright of all the stars. I'm basically the bottom rung of the fame totem pole."

"*Honey*! Don't talk about yourself like that. You're the brightest shining star in the world, and you know it. And that has nothing to do with how many people know who you are."

"I know *you* think so, but you're my mom. You don't see me like the rest of the world does."

"The rest of the world loves you too, angel. And if they don't, they're the ones missing out."

I finish with my braids and go to sit next to her on my bed. "I guess. It's just, the thing is, my online personality is bubbly and *breezy*, and yeah, people like that, but that's not the real me. The real me is clumsy and awkward and insanely shy. The real me gets rejected. Guys don't like the real me. Pair that with the fact that I'm not a serious actor, and Dalton's just going to think I'm this silly kid."

"Oh, Harper. Just because Jack Walsh couldn't see what a lucky guy he'd be to date you does not mean you're anything other than incredible and beautiful and amazing, okay? He's just one guy. What did I tell you that day after school?"

"You're not a teenager until you've gotten your heart broken at least once."

"Correct. Everyone needs to go through it. It doesn't make you any less lovable, it just makes you human."

"Maybe you're right."

"I'm definitely right. And another thing, this Dalton guy isn't any better than you just because he's a movie star. Celebrities are flashy and exciting and our culture worships them, but that doesn't mean they're special gods. They are not, I repeat, *not*, any more worthy than anybody else. Okay?"

"Okay." I feel her words reach my brain and send calming vibes throughout my nervous system. "I hear ya, Mom."

"Good. Now go be your remarkable, delightful self, and remember: it isn't your job to impress him. You're Harper Jessica Ambrose. It's *his* job to impress *you*."

She stands up and kisses me on the head just like she used to do when I was little and had a scraped knee. Sometimes I wish I could be off on my own in the world just doing my Harper thing, but I gotta admit, it feels good to have Mom and Dad on my team.

* * *

Hair is done and mom time is done, so that means it's outfit time. I want to look nice but not like I'm trying too hard, so a few days ago with Ellie I picked out a red floral-patterned flare dress from Urban Outfitters with really cute double straps. I pair it with black patent-leather Mary Janes and a blazer from Topshop because I once read somewhere that the Magic Castle has a strict, sort of formal dress code. Outfit, check.

Last but so, *so* far from least is makeup. I always have a lot of fun doing my makeup because there are so many different components to it, so much so that I end up feeling a little bit like an artist, which is awesome and actually pretty empowering. I'm a teenage girl, so naturally I don't have the clearest skin in the whole world. There's this idea in "girl world" that our skin has to be perfect, and that's probably because everyone's skin in magazines and on TV is picture-perfect flawless. But the truth is, most people struggle with some form of imperfection, and before they get photographed for a magazine they put on makeup. Then they get photoshopped later. And if that isn't happening, the person being photographed is most likely Beyoncé, and we should all be bowing down to her majesty anyway.

But what if Dalton doesn't think I'm pretty? The thought flashes into my mind like a lightning bolt; I can't help it. *Adam Levine's party was pretty dark. What if when he sees my skin in the light he thinks I'm a monster and changes his mind about me?* Ugh, there's no time for this self-sabotaging line of thinking! I stare myself down in the mirror and say, "Harper, you are a goddess. If Dalton doesn't think you're beautiful, skin and all, then he's a shallow moron and you'll move on. A guy's opinion does *not* affect your self-worth."

Then, to be safe, I do my makeup exactly as I did the night of Adam Levine's party (because hey, it worked, didn't it?), and add a layer of waterproof mascara in case Dalton does turn out to be a jerk. Knock on wood! Voilà, I'm makeup ready!

Oh, wait, I'm not just makeup ready, I'm *ready* ready. I've actually run out of date-preparation tasks. And yep, just as I dreaded, it is seven-thirty and time for me to start driving, which suddenly feels extremely scary. I've prepared my look to a tee, and if I'm being honest, I look simply baller, gummed-out hair chunk and all. But now I actually have to go and talk to the guy, and I have no idea what I'm going to say. What kinds of things should I talk about? What if I act like a total spaz? Normally when I'm super nervous to go to an event, I just bring Ellie along with me, and she always does the greatest job at calming me down. But this is a date, I can't just invite Ellie last minute. I mean, that would be ridiculous. Right? Right, Harper. You. Cannot. Bring. Ellie.

Just then there's an unexpected knock on the door at the top of the basement stairs.

"Harper!" my mom calls down. "There's someone here to see you!"

Dammit. My heart skips a beat. Did I get it wrong? Is Dalton actually here to pick me up? No, of course not, how would he have gotten my address? *Okay, Harper, take a breath,* I tell myself, *it's all good. Just go see who it is. No reason to panic.* I grab my keys and my black Balenciaga bag and head upstairs.

"Who is it?" I ask my mom, who has a disconcerting little smirk on her face as she lingers by the basement door.

"He's in the living room," she stage-whispers. "I told him you'd be right there." She looks me up and down and lets out a little whistle. "You look *fancy,* honey."

"Tell me who it is, is it Dalton? Is Dalton here?"

Before she gets a chance to answer, I hear a voice that is most definitely not Dalton.

"Hey, Harper."

I turn around toward the doorway and standing there is *Jack.* Not my soon-to-be date, but *Jack.*

"Jack. Hi? What're you doing here?" He's wearing a navy blue hoodie and a Nirvana T-shirt.

His cheeks get a little red as he meets my gaze. "Wow, Harper, you look amazing."

"Thanks." I'm super confused and a little stressed out—I always like to leave myself extra time when I'm going somewhere new, so I really should be in the car already en route to the Magic Castle. "So, what's up?"

"I got us tickets to see Ed Sheeran at the Troubadour. I was going to tell you today at school, but I thought it would be a cool surprise."

"That's awesome, Jack. When is it?"

"Tonight."

Tonight?

I pause, not wanting to hurt his feelings. "Jack . . . I can't go to-night. I have a date. That's what I'm on my way to go do right now, actually."

"Ah, of course." He's disappointed, majorly. "That's why you look so nice. I mean, you always look really nice, but you know what I mean. You look extra nice tonight."

"Thanks, Jack." There's an awkward silence and I can feel my mom hanging back, watching everything play out. This is too weird. I give her a wave and head out the front door, Jack trailing behind me. "I'm sorry, but I really gotta go. Let's find another time to see a show, okay?" I use the clicker to open the car door and start to back away.

"Ditch your date," he blurts.

"What?" I shake my head. "Don't be ridiculous, I like this guy."

"Harper, please, don't go. I hate the thought of you with some guy you barely even know."

"How do you know I barely know him? Look, Jack, you had your chance with me. This is all too little too late. I can't just drop my life just because you suddenly decide you're interested. And speaking of that, your interest feels very timely considering the fame I've found online. You never liked me when I was a nerdy nobody."

"That's not true."

"Right."

"No, really, how can you possibly think that? I've been trying to—"

I check my phone: 7:42. Crap. "Jack, I'm sorry, but I really have to go. We'll talk another time."

I give him a weak wave goodbye and roll up the window. I sit for a moment, mildly stunned, thinking, *What the hell just happened? And why do I feel so awful about it?* Then drive away.

* * *

During the drive I calm myself down and recenter myself for the night ahead. Like I said to Jack, it's nice he's decided he suddenly wants to be with me, but that ship has sailed. And it's headed right toward Dalton James. He's who I need to be focused on right now. I put on my best pump-up music and roll down the windows just a bit, not enough to mess with my hair but enough to feel wild and fancy-free. Let's get this started.

I parallel-park on a side street (without dinging any cars, thank you very much), and with slightly shaking legs begin walking toward the Magic Castle. I have never been more nervous in my whole life than when I am trudging up its majorly steep driveway (in heels, nonetheless). There are all these mega-fancy-looking people in tuxedoes and gowns, driving up in their Maseratis and Lamborghinis, and is it just me, or is everybody staring at me like I don't belong here and did it suddenly just get ten degrees warmer out here? Yep, they're definitely staring. If Ellie had been here, she'd grab me by the arm and say, "Babe, why you think the world revolves around you is beyond me. Nobody is even looking at you. Now for god's sake, snap out of it." Okay, I think, maybe I'll just imagine she's here with me. It's all good, Harper, you're blending right in; no one thinks you look out of place; no one thinks you're a loser and that you should go home. You deserve to be here just as much as anybody else does. You got this.

My heart is racing like a hummingbird's by the time I get to the front door, where a gaggle of women in white dresses are smoking cigarettes and a big, bald doorman stands watch with his arms crossed. I get a text from Dalton that says:

Tell the doorman you're meeting Dalton James.

I put my phone away and walk up to the doorman as confidently as I possibly can and say, "Hi, I'm meeting Dalton James."

Of course I'm expecting to be met with doubt and condescending laughter, but instead the doorman smiles and says, "Yes, Mr. James is expecting you. Right this way," and unclips a red velvet rope to let me through.

Next thing I know I'm in a dark room with bookcases from wall to wall and portraits of various famous magicians in big glass frames. There's another doorperson, this time a woman with bright red lipstick, who directs me to one of the bookcases and says, "The password is *open sesame*."

"The password?"

"Yes. You have to say it to get in."

"To get into the bookshelf?" I'm confused. And skeptical.

The woman sighs, impatient. "Just say it, miss."

"Uh, okay. Open sesame."

At this, the bookcase begins to vibrate and slide open. *What is this, Hogwarts?* I think to myself. Impressive. Also: *open sesame*? Seriously?

"Mr. James is just through the door. Enjoy your night." And with that, I'm thrust into a vast room filled with circular red dining tables and elaborate candelabras and of course Dalton, sitting at a table with a group of people who are all very put together and proper looking, not to mention at least two or three years older than Dalton and me. Everyone at the table looks super at ease in their environment, as if they've been here a million times before. One girl (woman?) is actually wearing a fur coat and pearls. She might as well have a cigarette holder and monocle to complete the ensemble.

"Harper!" Dalton hops up from his seat to meet me, leaning in for a cheek kiss. *Are my legs shaking?* I panic a little. *Yep, I think my legs are actually shaking.* I mean really, though, how could they *not* be at a time like this?

"I am so happy you're here. This is Jake, Roger, Diane, Angelica, and Lilly. Everyone, this is Harper." He shows me off proudly to the group, and I am met with unenthusiastic salutations. "Here, why don't you sit down and I'll go grab you a drink?"

"Actually," says the long-haired, British-accented one named Roger, whom I recognize as the lead singer of rock band the Wayward Donnellys, "the show starts five minutes from now, so let's just head over to the stage." Roger pushes his chair back and stands up, demonstrating how extremely tall and gangly he is.

"But I'm so comfy here," Angelica complains, brushing her curly blond hair away from her eyes. "Can't we just keep lounging? The thought of standing up again in these heels is enough to make me cry." Angelica is a model, I've seen her face in numerous Revlon ads.

"So dramatic!" Diane swats at her playfully. All three women are wearing 1920s imitation flapper dresses, and it's safe to say I don't fit in.

"Take those crazy shoes off, then. I told you not to wear them," Roger mumbles.

"Don't be such a grouch!" Angelica laughs at him. "It's your birthday, just relax. I'm only teasing anyway. I'm famished and totally ready for dinner. Let's go, let's go."

Dalton and I trail behind the group, following them down a hallway that is lined with a navy blue carpet and embroidered with golden moons. We enter a cavernous, antique-looking auditorium, where watery blue lights wash the audience chairs in an undersea glow. By the time we take our seats in the front row, my mouth is practically agape.

"I'm so excited that I get to take you here for your first time. I had some second thoughts about this place as a good first date, but then I just thought what the hell, you know?" Dalton has an excited, almost mischievous look in his eyes. "I come here as often as possible because it truly, genuinely blows my mind. The magic is so impressive. Especially this guy we're about to see. Bobby Bellarmine."

"Oh, I'm sure. I've actually always wanted to come here. Every time I drive by I just can't believe how . . . magical it looks. I mean, of course it looks magical, it's the Magic Castle, but I mean I can't believe a place so fantastical actually exists in Los Angeles. It looks like it should be in a fairy tale, not just like hanging out on Franklin Boulevard as if it's a normal building."

"You are so cute," he says. "I'm so happy you agreed to go out with me. I was worried you'd cancel last minute."

Dalton James thought *I* would flake out on *him*? What world was I living in? "What?! Why would I do that?"

"Well, who knows, I could be a psycho killer. Maybe you'd have been smart to cancel."

"A true psycho killer would never say something like that. What would be the point in telling me you're a psycho killer if you actually *are* a psycho killer? That would just scare me away and you wouldn't get a chance to do to me whatever psycho killers do."

"Well, kill, normally. Butcher. Bludgeon. That sort of thing."

"I think at this point I'm just going to have to trust that you aren't planning on butchering or bludgeoning me," I say.

"Whoa, this conversation got dark," he says, seeming a little flustered, "*Anyway*, thank you for meeting me. I'll work on making more normal and less creepy jokes."

Wait a minute! Is Dalton James socially awkward too? The way he's jabbering on it almost seems as if he might actually even be nervous to be on a date with me. Me! Little old me! This night is shaping up to be pretty interesting, and it's just getting started.

Suddenly the lights dim all the way until the room is pitch-black.

"Ooh, it's starting." Dalton lightly squeezes my shoulder in anticipation. A spotlight appears in the center of the stage and a short man with long black hair walks out in a smoking jacket and top hat.

"Ladies and gentlemen," the magician announces, his voice full of bravado and drama, "you came here tonight to see the impossible take place, to see the impossible become quite possible right before your very eyes." He wriggles his wrist and a deck of cards appears. The audience goes bananas. "Now, I'll need a quick volunteer. You, in the dress."

It's a good few seconds before I realize he's talking to me.

"Yes, you. I'm going to have you pick a number between one and five."

"Seven," I say too fast. By the time I realize my mistake it's too late. The whole room is roaring with laughter. "Oh god, I mean, uh, I mean three."

"Maybe a little less liquor for this one," the magician quips, prompting more laughter. I want to jump up and shout, "I'm not drunk, I'm just nervous!" but instead I keep my eyes to the ground, hiding my face from the world, so embarrassed I miss the rest of the trick.

"That was adorable," Dalton leans in and whispers in my ear.

"It was so embarrassing! I made myself look like a total ditz."

"That's not how I saw it," he says, kissing me quickly on the cheek. *Oh my god, did Dalton James just kiss me?!* For the first time, I understand the sentiment in books and on TV when characters newly kissed by their crush say, "I'll never wash my cheek/hand/other body part again!"

Then the show picks up and becomes truly magical. The magician hides a lemon in a thimble. He cuts a deck of cards in half and heals it back together with the power of his mind. He makes a parakeet disappear with the wave of his hand, then reappear, this time with a twin. He changes a card from an ace to a king just by flicking it with one finger, before he makes the same card change from black to glittery blue.

"That's impossible!" Dalton cries out. "Harper, did you see that? How'd he do it!" He's practically jumping out of his seat with excitement before he realizes what he's doing and slowly sits back down. "Okay, I'll stop making a fool of myself now."

"Not at all. It's cute," I say, and blush.

Dalton smiles at me almost shyly. "Now you know how I felt when you said 'seven.' "

After the show, it's time for dinner in the main dining hall. A waiter in all black wearing a red bow tie comes by to take our drink orders. Roger orders a scotch neat. Jake orders a Corona. Diane, Angelica, and Lilly order apple martinis. Then it's my turn.

"I'll have a Pellegrino, please," I say, "with lime. Thank you."

The waiter jots down the order and exits through swinging double doors.

"Pellegrino?" Roger says. "Dalton, she's almost as boring as you are."

"Shut up, Roger," Dalton says casually, like he's said it before a million times.

"Yeah, Roger, shut up," Lilly says, then turns to me. "Sorry about him. He's just not a very nice person."

I can't think of what to say to this, so I just shrug.

"So where'd you two meet, anyway?" Jake asks.

"A New Year's Eve party at the Chateau."

"Oh, *really*? Well, that's a change," says Jake.

"A change from what?" I ask. The waiter comes back effortlessly balancing all our drinks on a platter.

"He mostly picks up fangirls off the Internet."

"What the hell, man?" Dalton scowls.

"What did I say wrong?" Jake feigns innocence, but his eyes betray a guilty glimmer.

"Um, well, you just told my date that I pick up random girls all the time, for starters."

"Well, was I lying?" Jake challenges. Dalton is quiet. "Look, it's actually a good thing. Harper should be pleased, actually. I mean, my whole point was that she's obviously not just some random fangirl. She's classy and cool and means something to you. Otherwise you wouldn't have invited her to Roger's stupid birthday party."

"My party isn't stupid." Roger pouts, gulping down his beer.

"Look," I speak up and everybody seems to be surprised, "it's none of my business who Dalton has dated or is dating. I literally met him a week ago."

"Oh my god, I love that attitude," Diane gushes. "I like you, you're sweet."

"Thanks." I don't really know how to respond. I run my finger through the condensation on the glass of sparkling water sitting between Dalton and me.

"Okay, so tell us more about yourself." Jake leans his chin onto his palms. "We barely know anything about you."

"Yeah!" Angelica agrees. "What do you do?"

I can feel myself blush as the attention turns back to me. "Oh, ha, I'm one of those YouTube people."

"What does that mean?" asks Jake.

"One of what YouTube people?" asks Angelica.

"You like make videos and post them to YouTube?" asks Diane.

"Like, who doesn't make videos and post them to YouTube?" asks Lilly. Yep, like I mentioned, I get this a lot.

I'm gearing up to hit Lilly back with my usual response when Dalton chimes in. "It's actually really cool," he says. "She has a channel where—no, I'm sorry, you tell them! It's your life." His smile is warm and open and interested, not at all condescending or holier than thou, the way you expect celebrities to be.

"So, I have a channel where I post videos on, like, how to do makeup, or how to style yourself for different events—all kinds of do-it-yourself type videos too."

"And her channel has a million subscribers," Dalton adds proudly. *Awww, he's proud of me,* I think. *What a cutie pie*.

"Oh, I get it," says Roger with a majorly cynical tone in his voice. "You make silly videos of yourself putting on makeup and loads of people watch it, so next thing you know you have makeup companies paying you to say you use their products."

"Well—"

"And magazines write up little pieces on you and you get invited to all the coolest parties, and people call you an 'influencer,' so you think you're really important."

"Well, no—"

"And you end up hanging out with all these celebrities, so you start to think of yourself as a celebrity even though you're not an actress or a musician. You're just a girl who puts makeup on and expects to be treated as if you're talented."

"Excuse me, bro?" Dalton places his palms flat on the table. I have to admit, I'm on the verge of tears. Roger has successfully hit me where it hurts.

"What? I'm just stating my opinion. I think YouTube stars are total phonies."

"Why are you such an asshole, Roger? Did no one teach you how to be a civilized human being? And what's so legit about what you do? You've had minor roles in, like, two movies and live in your dad's garage. I mean—"

"Okay, that makes it sound like I live in an *actual* garage. It's a guest house, man. It's two stories."

"That is so far from the point, *man*. You're way out of line and I think you need to apologize."

"For thinking YouTube stars are phonies? No way, the whole thing is a total scam. She probably doesn't even use the products she promotes in her videos."

"All right, you know what?" Dalton pushes his chair out and stands up. "We don't have to stay here. Harper, let's go, I'm sorry about this *crap*." He glares at Roger. "Happy birthday, asshat." Then he grabs my hand and starts to lead me away from the group.

I give Roger a dirty glare and follow Dalton's lead.

Now, can you blame me for falling head over heels? I'd have to be crazy not to.

"Let's take my car and we'll come back for yours later. I'm so sorry about that, Harper," he says, opening the door to his black

Audi R8 for me and then jogging around to the other side. "I don't know what Roger's deal was tonight. He's normally not like that."

I slide onto the seat, relishing the feel of the plush leather, and lay a hand on Dalton's shoulder.

"You don't have to apologize for him. I'm actually really used to it."

He looks at me. "Used to jerks?"

"No. Well, yeah. But more specifically, people who are bitter about YouTube stars. Or think YouTube stars aren't deserving of success because we're not like real artists or whatever. This opinion is not uncommon, as it turns out."

"I don't get it. Why are they bitter? Hasn't anyone heard of a little thing called *Live and let live*? It's not like you claim to be an artist. Why does everything have to be art?"

"I know, right? Let's call a spade a spade! I make DIY videos, I'm not trying to reinvent the wheel. I just want to share what I know with the world, and people happen to like it."

"So why do people get bent out of shape about it?"

"I dunno."

"I think I know."

"Yeah?"

"Do you want to know what I think, honestly?"

"Honestly, yes."

"I think they're jealous."

"Jealous? Of what? We've already established that I'm not a real artist. Or even a fake artist. I'm actually not any kind of artist at all." The words leaving my mouth sound so ridiculous, I have to laugh at myself.

"Okay, well that's beside the point." He turns the car on and the leather seat starts to emit warmth from under my butt. Yummy. "The point is, you make a living doing what you love, and you're not even an adult yet. Do you realize how rare that is? I mean, even *I'm* a little bit jealous."

"*You* are?" My jaw practically hangs open. "I mean, you *are*?"

"Yeah, a little."

"But you've got the same thing going for you. You make a living doing what you love and you're not an adult yet either!"

"Well . . ."

"Well, what?" The more we talk, the more I feel myself loosening up around him.

Gradually it becomes almost comfortable to say what's on my mind.

He pauses for a minute as though he's not sure he wants to continue, and then he lets out a large breath. "I don't love acting anymore. Lately."

"That seems normal, right? To go through phases of not liking what you do? I mean, there are times where the last thing I want to do is make another video, but I push on for my fans. And then I love it again and it's all okay."

"I guess, sure, maybe. But I don't know, it doesn't make me happy anymore. It's depressing, actually. All I do is pretend to be someone else all day and then all of the world sees me and thinks I'm that person. Everyone assumes they know me, so they don't bother getting to know me. You saw what my friends are like—they don't know me, they've never taken the time."

"Forget those guys, though, you were right before when you said they're just jealous."

"Oh god, I've let the conversation get dark again. You must think I'm the most downer date of all time."

"No, I really don't. I'm having a nice night." *Better than nice,* I think to myself.

"Oh yeah? Nice? Well, you ain't seen nothing yet. Get ready for the night of your life."

"I was born ready," I say, and he smiles a sexy sideways half-smile, then turns up the volume on Explosions in the Sky as we race west on the 10 Freeway, swoop onto the Pacific Coast Highway, stars shimmering in the water to our left like they've fallen into the softly rolling waves and are too comfortable to pin themselves back to the sky.

Moonshadows is a restaurant and bar built on the small strip of land pressed between the Pacific Coast Highway and the ocean. The sign looms big out front, glowing bright blue. A hostess in patent leather pumps and impressively impeccable makeup leads us to the outdoor lounge, where Dalton has a table perpetually reserved.

Tables is a bit of a loose term for the seating scattered around the lounge. They're actually big cushy blue mats that might as well be small beds with drink trays rising out of the center. We recline into ours, which is right up against the glass barricade looking over the ocean, ink black and turbulent in a good way, romantic. Dalton orders us two Shirley Temples and a basket of mozzarella sticks and fries, which is honestly so far the highlight of the night, because to be quite honest (hashtag TBQH) I love, love, LOVE mozzarella sticks and fries. And as I slowly sip my Shirley Temple, I remember how much I used to love those as well. Shirley Temples are major hashtag TBT goals.

"For most of my life I thought the ocean was this made-up, mythical invention," Dalton says, breaking a french fry in half, then into thirds and sixths. It's the kind of thing I would do, actually. "I saw it in movies and on TV and stuff, but it seemed too good to be true."

"Oh my god, how old were you when you finally got to see it?"

"Fourteen, I think. And I've been in love with it ever since. Got a house in Malibu right on the beach, actually."

"Wow. That's . . . the life." *That's the life?* I sigh inwardly at myself. Well, maybe I'll never master the art of being cool around guys, but the good news is it doesn't seem to matter, because whatever I say only makes Dalton's smile light up even more, so maybe just being myself really is the way to go after all.

"It's a nice life. What about you? You must have gone to the beach practically every weekend as a kid."

I shake my head. "Honestly, no. We really took the beach for granted when I was a kid. I think my whole childhood I only went, like, three or four times. We didn't realize how lucky we were to have it close by."

"Oh, I would have killed to live near the beach as a kid."

"My dad used to always say, 'You know, we're really lucky to live near the beach. Most people have to pack up their cars and drive for miles if they want to see the ocean. Some people never get to see the ocean as long as they live,' and blah, blah, blah. But he barely ever actually took us because he has this weird fear of sand crabs."

"*Sand crabs?*" I can't tell if Dalton has no idea what sand crabs are or if he just can't believe a grown man would be afraid of them.

"Yeah, you know, those disgusting wriggly crabs that live under the wet sand that you can go digging for?"

"Yes, yes, I know what sand crabs are, but does your old man know he doesn't have to go digging for them? I mean, theoretically, if one never wanted to see a sand crab as long as he lived, this would be very easy to accomplish."

"Oh, tell me about it! It's totally ridiculous. He said he didn't feel safe just knowing they were nearby. Even if he couldn't see them. Now, mind you, he wasn't afraid of sharks, just sand crabs. Still is."

"Hilarious," Dalton says. "And what about you? Do you have any irrational fears?"

"Definitely. Lots, actually."

"Name one. No, name three."

"Three? Fine, okay. Let's see . . . So there's my fear of flying."

"That one's not so weird. Loads of people are afraid of airplanes. Especially after 9/11."

"Sure, but statistically you have a bigger chance of getting crushed to death by a vending machine than dying in a plane crash."

Dalton laughs. "Hey, don't make light of the danger that is vending machines. Would you want to get stuck under one? I wouldn't." He takes a sip of his drink. "What else ya got?"

"Okay . . . There's my fear of spiders, which you might say is common and understandable, but there is nothing common or understandable about the nature of my fear. Sure, I freak out if there's a spider nearby, but I can't even handle being around fake spiders, seeing pictures of spiders, or hearing stories about spiders. At the end of each day I search my hair and my clothes to make sure no spiders are hiding on me somewhere, even if I haven't been anywhere that spiders would theoretically be around that day."

"Okay, that's pretty intense. You've got one more."

"I saved the best for last."

"Okay, go."

"Tinfoil."

He almost spits out his mouthful of cheesy, gooey mozzarella wrapped in crispy breading. "*Tinfoil?* You're afraid of *tinfoil*? Why?"

I throw up my hands, as mystified as Dalton seems to be about that one. "I've never really figured out why. It's, like, is it metal? Is it paper? I don't trust it." That's it, Harper, let your freak flag fly.

"I don't think tinfoil is the sort of thing that requires trust. It just is what it is. It does its own . . . tinfoil kind of thing."

"Yeah, well, that's part of the problem for me. It's unpredictable! It looks harmless and boring, but then all of a sudden it can cut you out of nowhere."

"But, like, not very deep or anything. You might get a paper cut at the very worst."

"I also don't like the sound it makes," I admit.

"Tinfoil doesn't make sound!" He's visibly delighted at my wackiness and I'm proud of myself for opening up.

"It does! If you rub it against itself. It makes an awful scratching, scraping sound that has a weird tinny echo."

"But why would you rub two pieces of tinfoil together in the first place?" Dalton asks.

"Well, *I* wouldn't, but when I was in elementary school, kids would do that with their lunches. They'd collect all the tinfoil their parents used to wrap their sandwiches or apples or whatever, and they'd crunch it into balls and use the balls to play catch or to try to juggle. The balls would always bump against each other and make that awful sound. It's like nails on a chalkboard, only I don't think anyone else hears it that way."

"There isn't a chance you were attacked by these tinfoil balls in, let's say, a sort of dodgeball scenario, is there?" Dalton's eyes twinkle.

"How did you know?"

"There's clearly some deeper trauma involved than just an unpleasant sound."

"Elementary school kids can be so mean."

Dalton's voice drops a level as he wipes his hands on a cloth napkin and looks out at the ocean. "They were mean to me, too."

"Really? Even though you were already a well-known stage actor?"

"Are you kidding me? That made it so much worse. They called me 'pretty boy' and spread rumors that I wore makeup."

"Did you wear makeup?"

"Onstage only! It's part of the job."

"Fair enough."

"Hey! How did you know I used to be a stage actor? Have you been stalking me?" he teases, tucking my hair behind my ear so that my whole face is exposed, vulnerable. I have nothing to hide behind now.

"I, uh, well, small confession." I'm blushing harder than I've ever blushed before, but there's no turning back now. "When I was a kid my mom took me to see you in *Oliver Twist* when it was in New York."

"She did? That's incredible! I mean, I'm sorry you had to sit through that, but I absolutely love that you were there."

"You do?"

"Uh-huh, I only wish we had met that night. Think of all the wasted time! It's tragic, really."

"You were very talented, even back then. That was the year I first wanted to be an actress, and I remember just being in awe that you could perform that way in front of so many people."

"My god, you're beautiful, smart, *and* feeding into my ego. You better stop that or I'll fall madly in love with you."

We laugh, eyes locked in a magnetic pull. I hear my mom's voice in my head (*it's* his *job to impress* you) and coolly break the gaze.

"So what about you," I ask. "Any weird fears?"

"None. I'm a guy, guys don't have fears," he says jokingly.

"Oh, *sure*. Come on, I told you mine."

"If I tell you, you won't make fun of me? Or go telling Perez Hilton?"

"Oh my god, I would never."

"Okay." He leans forward and lowers his voice conspiratorially. "Did you ever see *The Brave Little Toaster*?"

"Yes."

"So there's this one scene where the toaster has a dream—actually it's a nightmare—that he's caught on fire."

"And the clown firefighter shows up!"

"Yes! You know what I'm talking about?"

"Of course. He's a firefighter, but his face is a clown's face, an evil clown's face, and he rises up out of nowhere really slow and ominous until he's looming over the Brave Little Toaster with his big evil clown face. Oh, and also it turns out he doesn't fight fire, he sprays fire out of his hose. Chilling."

"Yes! And then he looks down at the Brave Little Toaster and whispers—"

"*Run*," we say in unison.

"Oh my god, yes, no one has ever known what I'm talking about before," Dalton crows.

"I watched it a few years ago and could not believe how scary that scene was, like, it's insane that it's meant for kids."

"Exactly. That's what I'm saying. And then the Brave Little Toaster starts trying to run away from the evil clown firefighter, but there's this big tidal wave catching up with him, and the tidal wave starts morphing into a sea of forks trying to impale him, and—"

"And then suddenly he's hanging above the bathtub filled with water and trying to hang on, but he falls and gets electrocuted. Then he wakes up. That's pretty creepy stuff."

"I had a babysitter who played it for me once when I was four, and it freaked me out so badly I couldn't sleep for weeks. Then literally just last year I watched it again for the first time since then, thinking, *Well, of course I won't be scared of it now,* but I totally, *totally* was. I swear to God whenever I close my eyes I see that clown face and it chills me to my very core."

"Wow. A grown man afraid of a cartoon clown," I tease.

"A cartoon evil clown who sprays fire out of a hose. Do you think I'm totally lame? It's not too late for you to leave. I'll close my eyes to make it easy on us both." Dalton screws his eyes shut and leans his head back against the lounger. I roll my eyes good-naturedly. So dramatic, a true actor to his very core.

"I don't think you're totally lame. I think it's adorable."

Dalton opens his eyes and they blaze at me, rendering me speechless. "Hey, I have a question."

"Yes?"

"Can I kiss you?" His voice is soft, a small smile playing around that perfect mouth.

Oh my god, oh my god, I think, *here we go. Be cool, Harper, be cool.*

"Uh-huh." I smile and nod, biting my lip. He leans in and presses his lips gently against mine.

I can feel the blood drain from my head and my heart rate spike. Okay, I've made it sound really unpleasant, but it wasn't, it was amazing: time stood still and it was like we had been elevated into the starry sky, just us two. There was no high school or stupid Ashley Adler, there was no Jack Walsh or @ThatBitchHarper or any of the other girls Dalton had picked up at bars or whatever in the past. There was only us, only this moment suspended in time.

He kisses me lightly at first, then with more urgency, with his hands in my hair, with his hands holding firmly onto my shoulders, his lips kissing the icy sting of Sprite and grenadine onto my neck and ears, with—

"Excuse me?" a female voice says, and we look up to see three girls in uniform American Apparel spandex and stilettos. "Hi," the one in the middle—blond and sort of British sounding—says directly to Dalton. "Sorry to interrupt, but you look really familiar. Do I know you from somewhere? Did we meet once?"

"I don't know," he says, slightly annoyed, running a hand through his hair, "I think I just have one of those faces. People think they know me all the time."

"Wait, did you go to Brentside High School? In England?"

"No, but I had friends who went there."

"Unbelievable. I swear I remember you from back then. Maybe we were at the same party once or something. I'm Stephanie, and this is—"

"I'm sorry"—he interrupts her and I want to shout out HALLELUJAH—"but we're sort of in the middle of something. It was lovely speaking with you. Have a great night."

"Oh," British Blondie's face falls, defeated. "Okay, see ya." She grabs onto the elbow of one of her friends and teeters away, her nose in the air.

Dalton shakes his head back and forth disbelievingly. "Harper, I'm so sorry. That's so annoying."

"It's okay, I get it. Let's face the facts: you're a really big celebrity and people are always gonna want to come up and talk to you. I don't blame them, really, even if they are annoying."

"Well, fame fades. I'm hoping this isn't going to last forever. I'd like to know what it's like to go out and not be interrupted, and honestly I just wish they'd be up front and ask for a picture instead of pretending like they know me from somewhere."

"That was ridiculous!" I laugh and he joins me. "Do they do that a lot?"

"Yes! It's shocking. They actually pretend they don't know who I am, and come up with some plausible story about where we might have met. It's always something plausible, so I can't outright say no, I don't know you, because I actually might have met that girl at a party in high school. She obviously knows that I grew up in that neighborhood—thanks, Internet—so she asks if we met at a party, betting on the chance that her accent and name-dropping a neighborhood high school will make me see her as a nonthreatening peer, instead of a potentially dangerous fangirl."

"Dangerous?"

He nods seriously. "Oh yes, fangirls can be quite dangerous. Fanboys too, actually. We have to learn how to differentiate the good-intentioned fans from the psycho ones. The ones who want to send you locks of their hair and such. Stay away from those, for sure. And the thing is, it's always the ones who pretend you look familiar who end up being wacky."

"Really?"

"Yeah, think about it. If you're a normal, sane person, you don't have a problem with admitting up front that you are a fan and would like a picture or autograph. I mean, maybe you're going to choose to be respectful and not approach celebrities when they're on a date"—he gestures between the two of us—"but if you are going to approach, the sane thing to do is just be honest about your motives. It's always a bad sign if someone is pretending that you look familiar but can't quite place you."

"Not to play devil's advocate or anything, but isn't there a chance sometimes people actually just think you look familiar and don't know where from?"

"Totally possible, but unlikely. Two years ago that would be so much more realistic, but now that *Sacred* has blown up, my stupid face is plastered all over every major city on billboards and the sides of buses and on TV. And that girl was British. *Sacred* is even bigger over there. It's practically like the *Twilight* of England."

"Yikes. Good point."

His cheeks color a bit. "I hope that didn't sound insanely arrogant. I'm more embarrassed than proud to be famous for being a ghost in a supernatural love story for teenagers and Middle American housewives. No offense to teens or Middle American housewives, it's just not what I want to be remembered for."

"What do you want to be remembered for?" I ask thoughtfully.

"You know, I'm not sure exactly yet. I'm thinking of getting back into theater. Or doing something else, something more meaningful. I want people to remember me as someone who changed the world for the better. We all love *Sacred*, me included, but it ain't no world changer, that's for sure." He dips into the impressive and very authentic-sounding southern accent he uses on the show, reminding me just how talented an actor he actually is. He can do it all.

"That would be awesome, for you to get back into theater."

"Do you ever consider acting?"

"Oh, yeah, a little, I think it could be fun. But I'm way too shy."

"Shy? No you're not! You broadcast videos of yourself to millions of viewers on a regular basis!"

"That's different, trust me. I have control over those and I film them more or less all alone by myself, so I'm not actually performing in front of everyone. It's super easy to pretend like no one is watching me. I cannot imagine having a bunch of cameras and a crew watching. Or even worse, a whole audience of people. Oh my god, I would die. I don't know how you do it."

"Eh, that part is easy. I just focus on my craft and forget they're there."

"That seems . . . challenging." He has gone back to that intense way he was staring at me before, and it makes me lose my train of thought. My head goes blank. Again.

"Hey, wasn't I in the middle of kissing you?"

"Hey, yeah, I think you were."

"Why'd I stop doing that?"

"Some girls wanted to know where they knew you from."

"Damn those girls," he says, leaning back in. We kiss for a moment. Then he pulls away abruptly.

"Would it be crazy if I asked you to come back to my place? Not to sleep over or anything crazy like that, I just don't want the night to end yet. I'm really enjoying just . . . being with you."

Whoa, there. I'd be lying if I said this night was anything but straight out of a fairy tale, but a girl has got to keep a guy wanting more. And I'm just not that girl; things feel like they're moving fast, and while it's exciting, it's also a little scary. "It's getting late," I say. "I mean, I don't want the night to end, don't get me wrong, it's just—"

"Of course, a girl's gotta get her beauty rest."

"Exactly!" I say, relieved.

"I want to do this again, though, okay?"

"Definitely."

"Come on." He kisses me on the nose. "Let's get you home."

As we step out of Moonshadows, we are immediately swarmed by an attack of flashbulbs, blinding lights bursting in every direction.

"Dalton, over here! Dalton!" the paparazzi holler out, talking over one another in a chaotic mess that is awful but somehow, at the same time, totally thrilling.

"Jesus Christ," Dalton mutters, shielding his eyes with one hand. "I'm so sorry, Harper, follow me." I follow his lead as he ducks back into the restaurant, away from the noise and light. We walk into a darkish corner near the bathrooms. He takes out his cell phone and starts typing as he speaks.

"Normally I have them pull my car around so it's ready when I leave, but for some stupid reason I didn't think it would be a problem tonight. They must have gotten a tip."

"Maybe it was those British girls," I suggest, trying to be helpful.

"Probably." He hits send and slides his phone back into his pocket. "Okay, now they'll bring my car around right to the front. We just have to wait a few minutes."

"Hey, it's totally not a problem. This is actually my first real run-in with the paparazzi. Kind of cool."

"Oh, definitely." His eyes light up. "The first few times were so exhilarating. It was a bit of an addiction at first. Back in the day Christina and I used to call them and tell them where we were. Don't tell anyone that—it's so embarrassing."

"My lips are sealed." *He trusts me*, I think. *He likes telling me things about his life*. The feeling is so warm and pleasant that I don't even mind him mentioning his superstar ex-girlfriend Christina Rush.

His phone buzzes and he looks down, then grabs my hand. "All right, ready to go back out?"

"Sure, let's do it."

"Okay, just walk a little bit behind me; it will protect your eyes from the light. And feel free to just put a hand up. I'll guide you so you won't trip."

I nod and follow him out the front door for a second time.

"Dalton!" FLASH! FLASH! "Dalton, where've you been lately?" FLASH! FLASH! FLASH! "Dalton! Who are you with? Is this your girlfriend? Who are you, sweetheart? Can we have a smile, mystery girl?"

We duck into the Audi and slam the doors. As Dalton drives off, the flashes become distant and tinted by his dark window glass, but my heart rate stays up. *Way* up.

"Mystery girl," he repeats. "I like that for you. It fits."

"Yeah," I agree. "That was pretty awesome. Makes me sound a lot cooler than I actually am."

"Oh no, you're so wrong. You're the coolest."

"It's adorable that you think that, but I promise you I'm not."

"Well, you are in my eyes." *Swoon*. What's a girl to do?

He reaches over to grab my hand again, and holds it tightly while we drive.

When he drops me off at my car back at the Magic Castle, I'm sad to leave him, and it takes all my effort not to say this out loud.

"Wait, don't go," he fake-pleads, "stay with me. We'll stay up all night and get breakfast in the morning."

Reluctantly I shake my head. "My parents are pretty cool, but I do have a curfew."

"Ah yes, see, that's why I left my parents in London."

"Good call."

"Will I get to see you soon?"

"Very soon."

"Tomorrow?"

I have to laugh. "We'll see," I say, my best attempt at playing hard to get. I give him a little wave and get into my car.

I swear when I close the door there are hearts in his eyes. And mine.

TUTORIAL #4

A Perfect Day in My Life

What do you do after you've had the most perfect night ever? Well, you have to follow it with the most perfect day. What does that look like? you ask. Well, ask no further—or, um, look no further! Here is the play-by-play of one perfect day in the life of Harper Ambrose.

On the perfect day I have nowhere to be, and that means I'm sleeping until noon. No judgments!

When it's finally time to get up, I start the day by brushing my teeth and washing my face to get the blood flowing. then head to the kitchen for breakfast, which is the best part of my day. Quick shout-out to my cat mug, which is an important part of any perfect morning. So, normally I'd eat fruit or something healthy, but on a perfect day, that doesn't happen. On a perfect day there's really only one thing appropriate to eat for breakfast, and that is . . .

DOUGHNUTS!!!!!!!!

There they are, just sittin' on my table. I approach them cautiously; you never know how doughnuts are going to behave. Or rather, you never know how I am going to behave when put in front of doughnuts. Ohhhhh, they look good.

The weather has been warming up, so I love to eat my breakfast slash dessert slash doughnuts out on the balcony. I grab a blanket and my Microsoft Surface Pro 3, which basically just replaces my laptop, so I can do my daily stalking of people on social media—it's fun! Then I have a really important decision to make: which doughnut shall I eat first? The one with Cinnamon Toast Crunch on top or the one with Lucky Charms? And the winner is . . . LUCKY CHARMS! Yeah, I'll have to eat a salad for lunch, but it's totally worth it. Then I spend a little bit of time just reviewing my calendar (NOTHING going on today, I repeat NOTHING), checking up on important things like the weather and Instagram, then head back down to my lair and WHAT? My bed is magically made! Thanks, Mom.

Just kidding, I make my own bed. Sometimes.

I get dressed in whatever, because let's be honest, I'm not going to beat myself up over my outfit on a perfect day like today. I choose a lacy gray sundress, throw on some makeup (for fun!), and am out the door to conquer my day. Carpe the hell out of that diem, as they say.

So . . . who doesn't love shopping and Jamba Juice, am I right? Somehow on the days when I have nothing to do, I always end up at a mall. I don't want it to happen, but it does, so . . . I'm just not gonna fight it, you know? So I'm at this mall and it's literally a dead zone, like nobody is here and it feels like the apocalypse has happened and I'm the last one in the world. Hashtag not complaining.

Next it's aimless driving time. I like to pump up the jams while I cruise around town, top down, with no destination in mind. Since it is a nice day out, I stop at Urth Caffé to do a little outside late lunch/early dinner, because let's face it, food is life. Literally, we would die without it. Anndddd like I promised, I do get a salad. It's like not the healthiest salad ever, but you know what, this is MY day, and yummi-ness matters most.

Back at home I have no videos to edit, so I take a bath with my LUSH bath bombs because, gotta be honest, it's an addiction. I think I have like fifty. Currently. So I just take my makeup off while the bath fills up, then I drop in the bath bombs and watch them explode into colorful wonderlands of heaven.

To finish off the day, I get a nice glass of ice water with *crushed* ice, NOT cubed, then crawl into bed with my Surface to watch some Netflix and check out some other YouTube vlogs. Every day, even a perfect day, has to end sometime, so I finish it up with some light stretches and some heavy gratitude for the amazingness of the day, and then it's lights out! *Falls asleep dreaming of doughnuts and bath bombs*

Thanks for caring about my perfect day. You seriously rock.

You are my everything goals.

Lots of love, Harper

• •

CHAPTER 5

Just His Jamba Juice Flavor of the Week

It takes me all of Saturday and the first half of Sunday to film "A Perfect Day in My Life" because I keep messing up and having to start over. I'll be in the middle of filming and have a flash of memory from my night with Dalton at Moonshadows—our first kiss, the crispness of the starry sky, the way he begged me not to go—and I'll start to get giggly and next thing you know I'm in full-on blush mode and have to call "Cut!" On myself. I'm the actor *and* director of my videos. Yeah, it's like that.

Toward the end of a long and languid Saturday, I get an email from my agent, Buddy Silvern. It says:

Is it true you're dating Dalton James?

I roll my eyes and write back:

We went on one date. And how do you even know about that?

His response:

This is great publicity for you. Keep it up.

Well, not gonna argue with that.

A little while after noon on Sunday, I finally finish up and start looking through the footage before I start editing. Boy, do I look like one lovesick maniac. And hey, anyone would be after a night like that—am I right? I'm only human, people. So then there's just one question rolling around in my single-track mind: WHY THE HELL HASN'T HE TEXTED ME YET?

The phone dings and my heart skips a beat, then drops a bit when I check the screen. Ah, it's only Ellie.

ELLIE:

Smoothies? I have to hear all about night out with lover boy.

ME:

Get over here ASAP. I've been trying not to kiss and tell like a basic bitch amateur, but I'm caving. Must. Tell. Everything. Let's do Jamba Juice.

Ellie shows up not quite fifteen minutes later dressed in polished Kate Spade from head to toe, and I'd love to try to keep up with *Vogue*, Ellie's bible, but I just don't have it in me, so I keep my pajamas on and put my hair up into a high ponytail before we hit the nearest Jamba Juice, which just so happens to be on Larchmont, which just so happens to be the cutest street of all time.

"What are you gonna get?" Ellie looks up at the brightly colored menu board with one finger to her lips as if deep in the throes of some major decision-making.

"Strawberry Dreamin'," I say without so much as glancing at the menu. When it comes to smoothies, I know what I want. "You?"

"What? That's not a thing."

"Of course it's a thing."

"It's not on the menu."

"Duh. It's on the secret menu."

"Yeah, right." She squints at me, not sure if I'm telling the truth or trying to pull one over on her. Poor Ellie can be gullible from time to time, so she's right to at least try to be on guard. However, in this case, I happen to be telling the truth: there is, in fact, a Jamba Juice secret menu. You can get access to the Jamba Juice secret menu only if you're a very important person—no, an extremely important person (#EIP)—a member of the smoothie elite, if you will. Just kidding. In real life all you gotta do is work some summer shifts at your local Jamba Juice, which I did last year before my videos took off, *thank you very much*.

"I'm serious, Ellie. There's a menu only the employees get to see."

"That's ridiculous. I'm imagining like a secret society of card-carrying smoothie experts or something. The first rule of the Smoothie Club is don't talk about the Smoothie Club." She rolls her eyes and we both laugh.

"Fine," I say, "Suit yourself. Be basic."

"*Hey.* No basic shaming."

"Okay, okay, just order your damn smoothie."

She orders an Acai Berry Charger, and I order my Strawberry Dreamin'. The cashier—a middle-aged man with one ear pierced—nods knowingly at my order and asks us if we want to add a boost, which we do not.

"Told ya," I say smugly. "It's a thing."

"Wow," Ellie says, fake-mystified. "You learn something new every day!"

We sit outside in the gloriously warm sunlight and Ellie wants to know everything (I mean literally everything) about my date with Dalton.

"Okay, so I met him at the Magic Castle," I begin. "And we saw a really awesome show where—"

"No, no, back up. What were you wearing? What was *he* wearing? Did he hug you hello? Kiss? How did he introduce you to his friends?"

"Oh god."

"Yeah, I want *that* level of detail."

So it goes like that, me telling a small chunk of the story and Ellie insisting I rewind and deliver all the details. She lets me gloss over nothing. I am not exaggerating when I say that by the time I'm finished telling the story, the sun has set and I've started wishing I had thought to bring a jacket.

"I can't believe you didn't sleep with him," Ellie exclaims when I reach the end of the story.

"Of course I didn't," I protest, scandalized by her assumption that I would. "I'm sixteen, for Christ's sake."

"So what?"

"So I'm not going to just lose my virginity to some random guy just because we have a nice night together."

"Harper, how many times am I going to have to tell you this? Dalton James is not just *some guy*. How many people get to say they lost their virginity to an A-list celebrity? It's practically unheard of!"

"That might be true, but it doesn't mean it's what I want."

"Is it *not* what you want? Are you telling me you don't want to tap that ass?"

"Oh my god, Ellie, you're too much. Yes, duh, of course I want to . . . do more with him. But no way José was I going to do that on the first date. That's not my style."

"Not your style." She laughs. "How do you know it's not your style if you've never tried it?"

"As if you know anything about sex."

"I don't! That's why you were supposed to sleep with him and tell me all about it!"

"We were just having such a great night, I didn't want to do anything to mess it up. And he obviously didn't want to either. He didn't pressure me or anything. I mean, he did invite me back to his house, but just to stay up and talk."

"Girl, I know you're not that naive."

"You're right," I admit. "I'm not." We burst out laughing.

"Okay, but seriously, sex jokes aside, aren't you so happy I made you talk to him that night? I mean, look at you! You pushed yourself out of your comfort zone, got out of your head for like one second, and ended up having a great night. None of that would have been possible if you hadn't taken a chance. I'm seriously so proud of you."

"Aw! Thanks, Ellie. Couldn't have done it without you." We bump our empty Styrofoam smoothie cups together and the sound is not half as charming as it would have been if they were champagne glasses. Just then, my phone *whir-whooshes* with a notification from Twitter. Uh-oh, it's from @ThatBitchHarper. I know this can't be good.

@ThatBitchHarper: Harper thinks she's so special just because she went on one date with @DaltonJamesOfficial. Doesn't she know she's just his Jamba Juice flavor of the week? #WontLast.

My face falls. *Jamba Juice flavor of the week?* That can't be a coincidence.

"What's wrong, Harp?" Ellie asks.

"Twitter. It's, uh . . . it's that troll account again."

"Oh God, what did she say this time? Or he. Could be a he."

"Well, here," I say, turning my phone around for her to read the screen. I watch her face as she reads, looking for a hint that it could have been Ellie who wrote it, even though I don't actually think my friend would betray me that way. I think. Still, the more I consider it, it's hard not to be a little suspicious when the account has tweeted things only Ellie would know both times, and has been active *only* when I'm with Ellie. Which doesn't even make sense, because you'd think—if it *was* Ellie—that she'd tweet after we parted ways for the night. But if she did write it, she should win an Oscar, because her face betrays nothing.

"That's insane!" she exclaims when she's finished reading. "How could she or he know you're at Jamba Juice?! Nobody else is even here." We both look around at the empty store.

"Could it be a coincidence?"

"That seems remarkably unlikely. Why say Jamba Juice? It would have been easy to just say *flavor of the week*. That *is* the saying."

"Well, what about . . ." She looks around, lets her eyes settle briefly on the cashier, and lowers her voice dramatically. "Could it be him?"

"Are you serious?" I can't keep the annoyance out of my voice any longer. "What does some random Jamba Juice employee care about my life for? It's not a stranger, Ellie, it's someone I know. And someone who knows I'm at Jamba Juice right now."

"Wait, what are you saying?"

"I'm saying, only one person knows I'm here right now, and that's you. Only one person knew I had plans with Dalton, and that's you. Please help me to understand how @ThatBitchHarper could be anyone but you?" I regret the words as soon as they're out of my mouth, but once I've put my suspicions out into the open, there's no taking them back.

"Oh my god." Ellie looks like I've slapped her across the face. "I can't believe you think I could actually do something like this. Or *would* do something like this. Why on earth would I want to hurt you?"

"I don't know! I really can't even begin to figure it out. You tell me! Why are you doing this? What did I do to upset you?"

"Harper. This is ridiculous. What would my motive be? I have no motive!"

"Maybe you're jealous of me."

Ellie widens her eyes. "Excuse me?"

"Well, I'm an established YouTuber and you're just starting out. Maybe you resent me for being so much farther along than you are. Maybe you're jealous that I have sponsors and campaign deals and get invited to cool parties and you can barely hit ten thousand subscribers."

"What the hell, Harper, are you serious?" she sputters. "What's wrong with you? I—"

"Or is this about Dalton? The tweets started right after I met him. Is that it, do *you* want to date Dalton?"

"I'm the one who insisted you go talk to him! You know what, I don't need this. I don't know what your deal is, Harper, but you need to take a good hard look in the mirror and ask yourself what kind of friend you want to be, because whatever is going on right now is toxic and I don't want to be a part of it." She stands up and storms down the block, angrier than I've ever seen her.

Tears sting my eyes as my BFF exits my life. For a moment I'm tempted to go after her, but then I realize—she never once actually denied being behind the account, she just got super defensive and bounced. Nothing says guilty like not even bothering to proclaim your own innocence.

I know it might seem like I was jumping to conclusions by deciding Ellie was behind @ThatBitchHarper, but there's really no one else who could possibly have the info needed to write those tweets. It makes me incredibly sad, but I'd be a fool not to face the facts: nobody else knew I had a date with Dalton, and nobody else knew I was at Jamba Juice. Ergo, the girl I thought was my best friend secretly had it in for me. We have to learn how to protect ourselves in this world, and when someone hurts you, it's wisest not to give her the opportunity to do it again. Fool me once, shame on you; fool me twice, well, it ain't gonna happen.

But then there's the issue of the content of this last tweet. This is the second time it's been suggested that Dalton is a major player. Sure, the first suggestion was made by Wikipedia and the second by Ellie writing as @ThatBitchHarper, but I can't help but feel uneasy. After all, it's been almost two whole days since I've seen him, and still no text. Am I just a flavor of the week? If so, I better be a flavor off the secret menu, because the last thing I need right now is to feel unremarkable. I take out my phone and write to Dalton:

ME:
Hey, can we talk?

DALTON:
Uh-oh, trouble in paradise already?

ME:
We'll see.

CHAPTER 6

Pooh and Becks Do It All the Time

I drum my hands on the wheel as I drive to meet up with Dalton, feeling awful about what just happened with Ellie and awful about what might be about to happen with Dalton, that we could be over before we really even got started. Just major sucky feels all around. Being a teenage girl can be difficult for many reasons, but mostly because of the land mine that is called boys. The land mine of boys feels impossible to navigate without getting an arm or a leg blown off somewhere along the way. I'd love to make a video for my followers outlining some tips on and techniques for interacting with boys—how to play it cool, how to keep them wanting more—except I cannot make such a video because I HAVE NO IDEA WHAT I'M DOING WHEN IT COMES TO BOYS.

First there was Jack, whom I could not get to ask me out when I actually wanted him to, and now there's Dalton, who obviously likes me but might just be too famous for his own good. Or for my own good. I don't know the rules when it comes to boys, let alone famous boys. Am I supposed to be aloof? Am I supposed to make him think I'm out of his league? Make him work for it? I once read somewhere that men live for the chase. Does that mean I'm going to have to spend the rest of my life running away? Agh. Too. Many. Questions.

One thing I do know is this: when in doubt, trust yourself. Trust your instincts. It's an insult to yourself when you or anyone else tries to insist you should be any other way than how you actually are. You are you, and I can't tell what point there really is in trying to be any type of person you're not. Unless you're a psycho killer, in which case you should probably change who you are. Anyway, the point I'm trying to get to is this:

After a quick change of outfit (blue sundress with black and gold Steve Madden flats), I'm cruising up to the parking lot on Sunset Boulevard of the famously exclusive restaurant and bar Soho House, where we agreed to meet, and am suddenly filled with the sense that when it comes to Dalton, I have to be my truest, honest self. That way I'll be able to tell what kind of person he truly is. If he likes me for being me, then I know he's right for me. And if he doesn't, then he isn't, simple as that.

I'm feeling almost confident when I tell the concierge my name and that I'm here to see Dalton. She checks my name off a list and directs me to the elevator, which makes soothing beeping noises as it rises. This place is awesome—why don't I have a membership at Soho House? Then I could just walk right in, wouldn't have to deal with any of this "I'm meeting Dalton James" nonsense anymore.

Once on the penthouse level, I walk down the dark hallway of a million black-and-white photo-booth photos to the bar where Dalton is sitting in a huge booth that dwarfs him. He's drinking espresso with a gigantic stick of crystallized rock sugar sticking out of it.

"Harper! I'm so happy you're here." He stands up to kiss my cheek. "It's great to see you again." There's a sparkle in his eyes and I almost forget what I'm here to talk to him about. When I sit down opposite from him in the booth, it all comes flooding back.

"What did you want to talk about, love?"

"Okay, well, it's kind of complicated. And a little bit surreal. Well, no, you're a celebrity, you're probably used to this sort of thing."

"Okay, sounds intriguing. You have my attention."

"The night after I first met you, this happened." I take out my phone and show him the first tweet from @ThatBitchHarper.

"Ah, yes." He nods. "The Twitter trolls. Not as bad as the in-person trolls, but still pretty bad."

"Sure, yeah. A troll is no big deal. But then today there was this tweet." I show him the second one from today.

"Yikes. That's harsh," he says with a low whistle. "I'm sorry someone said that to you."

"But here's the thing. I was *in* Jamba Juice when this was tweeted. And I realized that only one person knew I was at Jamba Juice, and only one person knew when I first met you, and that was my friend Ellie. So I realized she was behind it and we got into this huge fight. The only thing is I can't figure out why she would do this. It's such an immature thing to do, you know?"

"How bizarre." He looks at the phone, then at me, then at the phone, then at me, as if trying to figure out whether I'm crazy or not.

"I'm not crazy," I say. Smooth, real smooth.

"I don't think that you are. I just don't know what to make of all this. I've had plenty of Twitter trolls, but this has to be the strangest. Well, no, the strangest was when some girl started tweeting that I was a hermaphrodite and said she had pictures to prove it. The pictures were photoshopped, I swear."

"Yeah, no, I believe you." I laughed weakly. "Here's the thing." My inner self speaks up and I let her take charge. "I really like you. I had a great time the other night. But I don't want to date a player. And I don't want to change you, either. I'm not saying I need you to commit to me—I mean, we've been on only one date; that would be ridiculous and way too soon. All I'm saying is that if you're planning on dating me while also sleeping with all of Hollywood, I think we should just end it now. I just want to know what you're looking for."

Dalton is silent for a long moment as he swirls the crystal in his drink. "I see," he says slowly, at length.

"It's totally fine. I don't want to make you be anyone you're not or do anything you don't want to do. We had a really nice night and I don't regret any part of it. I think that you're—"

"Harper"—he puts his hand on my hand—"you're tripping."

"Yes. Yes, I am."

"Well, don't. Listen, yes, what they say on the Internet is true. I have a reputation for being a playboy and a bit of a flirt. I admit I wasn't a good boyfriend to Jade or Christina—I mean, they've both done a thorough job making sure all of the world knows that—but hell, I deserved it. I've been working on myself a lot and kind of just growing up. I think I'm already a lot less childish than I used to be. I don't want to be a player. I'm not interested in playing around anymore, actually."

"Oh."

"I was a bad boyfriend because I was young and stupid. And because I knew those girls weren't right for me. It never felt . . . right. You feel right to me."

"Oh." I mentally whack myself on the head for being so inarticulate and awkward, but I'm honestly floored by everything he's saying. It's pretty much the opposite of what I was expecting to hear.

"This might seem kind of intense, but I really want to do this. I mean, I want a relationship. I know we just met, but you're the one I've been looking for. It feels real, right? Don't you feel that?"

Wow. This was *really* not how I was expecting this conversation to go. Like at all. I figured once I spoke my heart and mind to him, he would go running in the other direction, straight into the nearest strip club or Victoria's Secret fashion show or wherever rich and famous playboy types like to hang out.

"Harper? Hello?" I guess there had been a few moments of my staring incredulously and silently at him.

"Yeah, hey, what's up?"

"Did you hear what I said?"

"Yes. But I don't believe it. You want to, like . . . be in a relationship?"

"Pretty much." He smiles shyly, like he's caught off guard by his own bold gesture.

"You want me to be your girlfriend," I say slowly.

"Yes."

"And you want to be my . . . boyfriend."

"Yes."

"But . . . But . . ." When something seems too good to be true, that normally means it is, right? I feel like at any minute I'll wake up from the happiest dream of my life and be thrust back into the cold, hard reality where Dalton James has no interest in a lowly YouTube personality like me.

"But what? Is that not what you want? We don't have to. I just like you so much and I can't think of anyone else I'd rather—"

"It is what I want. This is definitely what I want." I try not to sound too enthusiastic, but I feel like freaking Cinderella and he can probably tell. He leans in to kiss me, and as our lips touch, I feel my worries and fears just melt away. Boy has that effect on me.

"Listen," Dalton James, my new boyfriend, says, "I have to go to London next week for a few days. For work."

"Oh, okay," I say, somewhat disappointed. But my boyfriend is an A-list celebrity, after all. I suppose it comes with the territory.

"I think you should come with me."

"What? Me? Go to London?"

"Yes, is that too crazy?"

"Yeah! I mean, no, it's not *too* crazy. It's definitely a little crazy, though. I have school."

"So just come with me when I leave on Friday and stay for

Saturday and Sunday. Then fly back to Los Angeles on Monday. I'll have to stay for some interviews, then fly to New York for *The Tonight Show* with Jimmy Fallon."

"Okay, now you're losing it. Fly to England just for the weekend?!"

"Yeah, so what? Posh and Becks do it all the time."

"Posh and Becks?" I actually laugh out loud. "As in Posh Spice and David Beckham? Do I look like Posh Spice and are you David Beckham?"

"Well, no, but if they can do it, we can do it. It's not like you'd have to spend any money, you know? I'll get your ticket, and when we get there I'll book you your own room at the Kensington Hotel, on me. Whaddya say?"

"Oh, wow. Well, I'm in, but I can get my own ticket. And my own hotel room, actually."

"Are you sure? They're really expensive and I want you to sit with me up in first class."

"Yeah, I know. I got it."

"You can afford a first-class round-trip to London?"

"Hell yeah, I can." I grin. "Welcome to the life of a YouTube star."

I would never call myself that in front of anyone else, but hey, it's Dalton James. I survey his face, and VICTORY, he is effectively impressed.

"Hey," he says, "I just have one question."

"Go for it."

"If your Twitter troll really is this girl Ellie, why would she tweet about Jamba Juice while you were in Jamba Juice? Wouldn't that just make her extremely obvious and give away her cover too easily?"

That icky feeling I had in the pit of my stomach after Ellie stormed out of Jamba Juice starts to creep back up again. "Well, sure."

"I just don't get why she'd do that. If it really was her, you'd think exposing herself like that would be the last thing she'd want to do, in which case Jamba Juice would be the last place she'd tweet about."

"So then it's just an insane coincidence?"

"Maybe. But I think it's more likely that it's someone who wanted you to think that it was Ellie. Someone who wants to come between you two and tear you apart."

Oh, dammit, I think, *he's right, isn't he*? I think of the nasty things I said to her and feel literally like a subpar human. Ellie has always been a good friend, and at the first potential sign of trouble I turned around and treated her like garbage. Not cool, Harper.

So if @ThatBitchHarper isn't Ellie, then first of all, I have some serious apologizing to do. And second of all, I'm back to square one on finding out who this Twitter troll really is. Welcome to the *real* life of a YouTube star.

On my drive home, I call Ellie at least three times, but she doesn't pick up. Dammit, how could I be so stupid? After the way I jumped to conclusions, she'll never forgive me, and I don't blame her. I call one more time and this time I leave a message:

Ellie! It's Harper. I know you're not my Twitter troll and I am so profoundly sorry for accusing you. I don't know what I was thinking, I must have lost my mind for a second there. You must totally hate me right now, and I guess I would hate me too if I were you. I feel awful. I would do anything to fix this. All right. Bye for now. I love you.

Ugh. This is the absolute worst. As soon as I'm home I text her:

Ellie, I'm so sorry. Please call me.

She writes back immediately:

Not now, I need space.

She needs space? How much space? And for how long? My heart rate rises, and I'm getting kind of panicky. This whole thing feels totally out of my control and I don't like it one bit. There's absolutely nothing I can do right now except give her space. I mean, that's the right thing to do, right? Right. I click on my TV and try to zone out, but the sick feeling in the pit of my stomach won't go away and the truth keeps creeping up: I've been a horrible, horrible friend. Feeling depressed, I send a quick email to my agent:

Going to London on Friday, be back Monday, is that cool?

And then curl into bed and fall asleep before the sun has even set.

CHAPTER 7

A Tale of Two Parties

At lunch the next day I sit down with the Jessicas, a look of regret and self-loathing plastered across my face. I should be pumped about London, and don't get me wrong, I am, but the excitement is being almost completely eclipsed by my guilt about Ellie.

"Yikes, Harper, are you okay?" Jessa asks. "You look . . . exhausted."

"Where've you been?" Jessie adds, "I feel like we haven't seen you in forever."

She's right, it practically has been forever since I last saw the Jessicas. Last time I saw the Jessicas I hadn't yet gone on a date with Dalton James. That was a lifetime ago, a "forever" ago, as far as I'm concerned.

"I've, um . . . I haven't slept a lot. A lot has happened this weekend, you guys."

"Like what? You can tell us."

"Okay, but you have to promise not to freak out, okay?"

"We promise," they say in unison.

"I went on a date with Dalton James, and well . . . now he's my boyfriend."

"*What?!*" gasps Jessa.

"The *movie star*?" Jess gawks.

"Shut up! I don't believe you," groans Jessie. "Okay, fine, I believe you, but I'm practically dead of jealousy."

"Yep. We had an amazing night and things just sort of . . . moved fast, I guess." My eyes brighten and lighten at the memories of that magical night. "He invited me to go to London with him this weekend. I think I'm going to go."

"That is unbelievable," says Jessa.

"Then wait, why do you look so miserable?" asks Jess.

"Yeah, if I were you, I'd be over the moon right now," adds Jessie.

"All of that is the good news. The bad news is that I have a Twitter troll."

"No offense, but don't you have a million Twitter trolls?" asks Jessa.

"Well, yeah, but this one is different. It's someone *who knows me*, like, *in real life*. I think this one might be serious."

"What's a Twitter troll?" asks Jessie.

"Honestly, Jessie?" Jessa frowns. "It's someone who bullies you on Twitter."

"She calls herself @ThatBitchHarper and she's trying to ruin whatever this thing is I have going on with Dalton."

"Who would do that?" asks Jessie.

"I don't know, that's the thing. It's someone who knows me and my life, it has to be. I had reason to think it was my friend Ellie. I actually accused her of being behind it all; then I realized she couldn't have been. Oh my god, I'm such an idiot. If I was her, I'd never talk to me again. I feel terrible. It kept me up all last night."

"Okay, whoa, hold on," says Jessie. "You're being really hard on yourself. Someone is trying to tear you down and you don't know who it is, so it makes sense that you got a little paranoid, who wouldn't?"

"You're in a really weird situation, Harper," says Jess. "Like, this is not normal sixteen-year-old girl stuff."

"Tell me about it."

"You know what you need?" Jessa peps up then. "You need some good old-fashioned high school antics to put things in perspective, take your mind off of all this insanity."

"Oh yeah? What do you have in mind?"

"Clayton Schaeffer's parents are out of town tonight and he's having a party. I say we give you a dose of that good old high school life and show you what you're missing."

Party 1

The Jessicas had good intentions dragging me to this party, I know they did, but there's a reason I haven't been to a high school party in a long time: I hate high school parties. I don't fit in at high school parties; I feel awkward as hell at high school parties. I guess the reason I agreed to go along is that I felt desperate for a change of scenery, anything that might help me stop feeling like both victim and monster, anything that might help me feel normal.

When we show up at nine p.m. in Jessa's baby-blue 2001 VW Beetle, Clayton's poor parents' house is well on its way to being majorly trashed. Practically all of my peers are gathered around the dining room table playing beer pong, tossing white, light-as-air balls into red plastic cups of cheap beer, which splashes and spills all over the place each time someone decides on a refill, dripping down the table legs and soaking into the carpet while everybody hoots and hollers like cave people. No offense to cave people—they probably don't deserve this comparison. They didn't play beer pong, after all.

In the living room, Calvin Harris is blasting so loud I can feel it in my bones, and Calvin Harris is definitely not something I want to feel in my bones. They've turned the living room into a dance floor and are grinding up against each other like snakes in a pit. I feel dirty just watching them. Some of my peers are smoking near the open windows, but the wind keeps blowing the smoke back into the room so that the air is thick with tobacco and nicotine.

"See?" Jessa screams over the music. "Just regular people having a regular good time."

I look at her like she's crazy. If this is regular, then please, PLEASE, show me irregular. If this is normal, show me bizarre.

Out of the corner of my eye I see a group of my classmates whom I vaguely recognize from the hallways sort of leering at me.

They're looking at their phones, then looking back up at me. *Oh God*, I think, *this can't be good*.

"Excuse me." I break from the Jessicas to approach this group of Aéropostale-wearing morons. "Can I help you?"

"Sure," Ashley Adler swoops in. Dammit, there's so much smoke in the room I didn't see her there. "You can tell us about how you got into the world of naked modeling."

"What? I have never in my life—"

"Benji, show her." Ashley nods to Benji, who looks like his mom dressed him five years ago and he's been in the same outfit ever since. Benji turns his phone so I can see and my jaw drops so far to the floor that it might as well have been broken off my face. The picture I'm looking at is of my face photoshopped onto a naked girl's body.

"That's not me! It's so obviously fake."

"Doesn't look fake to me," Ashley snickers.

"And what? You're such an expert?" Normally I ain't no holla-back girl, but I'm in fight-or-flight mode now and my blood is boiling.

"Nothing to be ashamed of, Harper, it's not uncommon for D-list celebrities to try and get some attention with a naked photo shoot."

"Oh, give me a break, Ashley, I'm *sixteen*. Besides the fact that I would *never* do something like this, it would be completely illegal."

"As if there aren't tons of perverts out there who break that law on a daily basis."

"You're disgusting," I snap, on the verge of tears.

"Um, I'm not the one with naked pictures on the Internet."

"For all I know, you're the one who made this picture! I don't know why you hate me so much, I don't know what I ever did to you, but—ugh, you know what? Forget it. I don't have the energy."

With tears stinging my cheeks, I turn and make a dash for the front door.

"Harper!" It's Jessie, just barely catching up with me at the door. "Where are you going? Don't go, we just got here."

"I'm sorry, Jessie, I know you guys thought it would be good for me to come out tonight, but I can't be here. This isn't for me. Besides, you guys are the only ones who actually want me here. I'll see you tomorrow, okay?" *Not only did this party not make me feel normal*, I think, *it made me feel like an absolute alien freak*.

"Take me with you!" she blurts, her voice squeaky, almost desperate.

"What?"

"I don't want to be here either. I hate these parties. I hate the smell of smoke and stale beer and body odor. Please, I gotta get out of here."

Party 2

And that's how I ended up in an Uber with Jessica "Jessie" Dole headed to an address in the Hollywood Hills where Dalton said to meet him for an exclusive Hollywood party that "should be pretty chill."

"I can't believe I'm going to meet Dalton James!" Jessie gushes as we pull up to the Spanish Colonial Revival mansion just off Mulholland.

"You're probably about to meet a lot of other famous people too, so you might wanna reign in the fangirl vibes."

"Oh, don't worry, Harper, I promise not to embarrass you. I'll be cool."

"Thanks, Jessie, I'm counting on it," I say, then am suddenly hit with a realization, a change of heart. "Actually, don't worry about it, be as embarrassing as you want to be, they're just people, not gods. Let them think what they want."

So we strut into the party like we own the place, laughing and waving to total strangers, pretending like we've known them for ages, like we go way back. The party is smallish, almost intimate, and very high end. Dare I say . . . sophisticated? Everyone is wearing Rag & Bone and drinking red wine and Ray Charles is playing soft and crisp from sleek speakers in every room.

"This is . . . delightful." Jessie squeezes my arm. "Ohmygod, look, it's Kristen Stewart. And ohmygod, ohmygod, Harper, it's Sophia Wingate from the Disney Channel! She's talking to Dalton!"

"Come on." I laugh. "Let's go say hi."

"I can't. I'll totally lose it."

"So lose it, who cares? Worst-case scenario, you'll make me look cool, calm, and collected in comparison." I wink and lead her to Dalton and Sophia Wingate, who is wearing a gorgeous red cashmere sweater and black leather skirt. I love it when celebrities are even prettier IRL.

"Hi, babe!" Dalton pulls me in for a kiss and it makes me happy that he's not afraid to be seen with me.

I introduce him to Jessie and he kisses her hand like a gentleman, making her blush, then introduces us to Sophia, who is flattered when Jessie says "I've been obsessed with you since elementary school."

"Harper, hi!" It's Lilly and Angelica, the girls I met at Magic Castle, swooping over in furs and diamonds and pearls like two majestic birds.

"Harper, you remember Lilly and Angelica," says Dalton.

"Of course."

"I am so sorry about what a jerk Roger was last time we saw you," says Lilly.

"I've broken up with him since," says Angelica.

"It's really okay," I tell them. "I survived."

"Honey, were you crying?" Lilly asks. "Your eyes look red."

"Oh, ha"—I wipe my eyes, suddenly very self-conscious—"we were at a horrible party before this."

"*Horrible*," Jessie emphasizes.

"Bad enough to cry over?" Angelica asks.

"Yes." Jessie doesn't miss a beat. "These idiot kids were passing around a fake picture of Harper naked."

My cheeks burn, embarrassed.

"It was photoshopped, honestly," I try to explain.

"*What?*" Dalton almost spits out his drink. "Who are these wankers? I'll slap them!"

"Oh, um," I say, "just some kids from school, but I'm moving past it. No need to hit anybody."

"Welcome to fame, sweetie." Sophia gives me a sympathetic look with her famously angelic baby face.

"Has this happened to you?" I ask, feeling safe for the first time tonight.

"Duh! Are you kidding? I've been dealing with that insanity for as long as I've been on TV."

"I'm ashamed for society to say that it's happened to me as well." Dalton pretend-sulks.

"It happens to anyone who's anyone," Angelica says. "You're in good company, I promise. It's just an occupational hazard."

"It's never happened to me." Lilly pouts.

"Well, honey, you haven't made it yet," Angelica teases. "One day if you work hard enough and keep aiming for the stars, maybe you too will be lucky enough to have some creep superimpose your face onto someone else's body."

"Whose house is this anyway?" Jessie asks once we're all crammed into a titanium photo booth set up in the backyard.

FLASH!

The first flash goes off before we're ready and we laugh, slightly blinded by the light.

"It's my friend January's," says Sophia.

FLASH!

"January *Jones*?" Jessie asks, so clearly having the time of her life.

"Yeah, she's renting it from this guy who's renting it from Mark Zuckerberg, who just bought it from some Russian oil tycoon."

FLASH!

"Well, you don't hear that every day," I say as we all scurry to switch poses in time before the final FLASH!

"I'll get it, I'll get it!" Jessie is first to jump out of the booth and wait patiently by the photo dispenser.

"I like your friend, Harper. She's got good vibes," Sophia says, climbing out after her, and Jessie almost dies.

"I agree," says Angelica, holding up her wineglass. "Cheers to Harper and Jessie."

"To Harper and Jessie!" Everyone clinks glasses and Jessie looks over at me like *Oh my god, what is happening?*

"You know what we should do?" Lilly proposes. "We should jump in the pool."

"Are you high?" Angelica laughs.

"No! I'm just in a good mood. Can't I be in a good mood?"

"Let's do it!" Jessie cheers.

"I don't have a bathing suit," I say. "And I'm not about to get naked after the night I've had."

"So we'll go in our clothes!" Now Dalton is as revved up about the idea as Lilly and Jessie are; he's pulling off his leather jacket as he speaks.

"I'm game," says Sophia, taking off her cashmere sweater to reveal a pearlescent white tee.

"No way." Angelica crosses her arms. "I'm not wearing one thing that costs less than two hundred dollars."

"Oh my god, you're such a brat!" Lilly squeals.

"Yeah, right, those jeans are Brandy Melville and you know it." Sophia laughs.

"So what if they are? I'm not jumping. The last thing I need is to catch pneumonia."

"Suit yourself!" Lilly says, running and jumping feetfirst, jewelry and all. A pink glow emanates from the bottom of the pool and it looks pretty damn appealing.

Dalton and Sophia and Jessie follow her lead, making a huge splash.

"It's bloody cold!" Dalton hollers. "Can't Mark Zuckerberg afford to heat his pool?"

"Don't listen to him, the water's lovely!" Lilly calls out to Angelica and me, who gaze skeptically into the pool where the four of them are now treading water like a bunch of wet dogs. Truth be told, they look like they're having a blast.

"It's warming up now, actually," Dalton says. "Hm, I could get used to this!"

"Come on!" Jessie splashes us. "Get in here, get in here!"

Angelica and I glance at each other, like *Should we do this? Can we do this?*

"YOLO?" she says to me, with a slightly pained look on her face.

"YOLO," I agree. We clasp hands, and on the count of three, we jump.

"The other Jessicas are going to be so insanely jealous." Jessie, wrapped in one of Mark Zuckerberg's towels, is swooning in the backseat of our homeward-bound Uber.

"I'm glad you had fun," I say. My teeth are chattering and my

lips are practically blue, but I'm feeling satisfied and relaxed like never before.

"We should never have dragged you to Clayton Schaeffer's house. You're a big fish in a small pond there. You've got much cooler stuff going on, Harper!"

"Well, I mean, I've never really fit in with—"

"You were so right," she rambles on excitedly, "high school parties are not your scene. Those kids are small, close-minded, insecure little idiots. You should be hanging out with open-minded, worldly, creative people, like Sophia Wingate. People who get you and have real lives of their own so they're not just jealously trying to tear you down all the time. I'm telling you, Harper, Ashley Adler is so obviously dying of jealousy. Your success literally kills her, I can tell."

"Oh" is all I can say. For the first time I actually feel sad for Ashley Adler. Like any truly mean person, she must be really suffering inside. I look out the window at the city lights racing by and sigh. In the midst of being bullied, I had never stopped to consider what makes people mean. Nobody is born mean. People become mean when they're not given the love and affection they deserve; people become mean when they don't like themselves and just don't know how to handle that. Meanness comes from a place of deep sadness, no doubt. I had always thought Ashley just hated me, but now, with my cheek pressed up against the window glass, I realized it wasn't me she hated, but herself. The thought made me heavy. Didn't she have anyone to tell her she's awesome? Did she never have anyone to believe in her? Suddenly I stopped feel-

ing like her victim and started feeling like the lucky one: I may not ever be able to escape hateful people (i.e., the #haters), and they may always exist out there in the world, but as long as I'm kind to others and true to myself, at the end of the day, I'll always have my people waiting for me with open arms. I wondered if there was anything I could do to help her. Like always, I found myself wanting more than anything else to talk to Ellie, and crushed that I couldn't.

TUTORIAL #5

What to Pack for Vacation!

Here are some tips and tricks to pack like a pro:

1. So before I even start packing, I like to make a list of everything I'm going to need on my vacation and what I'll want with me on the airplane. So I'll go on Pinterest for inspo, because they have awesome lists on everything you could think of.
2. Check your closet and see what you actually do have in your wardrobe. I don't know about you, but I actually forget what I have and then I get all stressed, like, *Aaah, I don't have anything!* and then I go shopping and spend money and then later I realize I actually had a lot of good stuff and spent money for no reason! Yeah, it's good to check beforehand, trust me.
3. My third tip is to lay everything out on your bed before putting it in your suitcase. That way you can see what you're actually packing, which will hopefully prevent overpacking. Or underpacking, if that's an issue for you. Personally, I've never come close to underpacking even once in my life.
4. So then it's on to what to actually pack for your vacation. It depends on where you're going, but if you're going somewhere hot, then obviously I would suggest a couple of pairs of shorts, a few breezy tank tops for beach lounging, a selection of dressy/cute tops for fancier dates (just in case you meet BAE surfside, of course), and some short skirts. Even if you are in fact going

somewhere hot, I really recommend bringing your snuggliest sweater for when the sun goes down, as temps can get real chilly real quick. And then of course some dresses to wear to dinner or just to the beach to put over your bathing suit. And of course don't forget your jammies to sleep in. Am I the only one who loves that word? Jammies! It's such a cute word!

If you're not going somewhere warm, make sure to pack some pants or leggings (or both!). When it comes to shoes, I like to bring two or three pairs—sometimes four, just to be safe. If you bring something open-toed, also include something close-toed, and something with a heel, so you're pretty much prepared for any situation your vacation might throw at you.

5. Bring laundry bags or a wet clothing bag for your bathing suits. You're also going to want to pack your toiletries, of course, so what I do is lay them all out on my bed like I did with my clothes, just to see what I have. You're going to need the basics like shampoo, conditioner, soap, razors, toothbrush, deodorant, makeup wipes, and then also any makeup you might want to bring. I suggest some waterproof mascara for poolside chillin' (or rainy days!).
6. My final tip is to put some bright, easily identifiable tags on your luggage, especially if your luggage pieces themselves are sort of standard. The last thing you need after a long flight is a battle with some stranger over whose black Samsonite is whose. Trust me.

Extra Tip: On to what to bring in your carry-on bag: I pack my carry-on to the max, like, not a joke. I've had bad experiences where my luggage got lost and I've had nothing, so now to be safe I like to basically have my whole life with me in my carry-on bag just in case. I bring all my electronics, any headphones or chargers that I need, then also a notebook and some magazines to entertain me on my journey. Less exciting but super important are your travel documents, which you gotta have: boarding passes, passport (if you're traveling internationally), wallet, ID card, money, et cetera et cetera. Last but not least, I like to bring snacks slash candy onto the plane with me—and gum! That's what keeps me going on a flight, and what keeps my ears from popping out of my head during the ascent and descent.

So that is pretty much it for this vacation essentials tutorial! I hope you guys can now pack like a pro and are so excited for any vacations you've got planned. I'll see ya on the flip side!

You are my everything goals.

Lots of love, Harper

CHAPTER 8

Suspects

If two weeks ago you had told me that I'd be sitting next to Dalton James on a Virgin Atlantic first-class flight to London, I would have laughed in your face. I mean, come on, life just doesn't work like that. At least I'm not used to life working like that, anyway. That's how I know this is meant to be; without fate or a higher power, something like this could never happen. At least that's what I told my parents when pitching them the idea. After about seven hours of begging and what felt like an eternity of their deliberating, they finally agreed to let me go, with the condition that I call them once a day (fine), don't do drugs (duh), and promise to practice safe sex (duh!). To borrow a line from one of my biggest role models, Cher Horowitz, aka Alicia Silverstone in *Clueless*: AS IF! Dalton and I just met, sure we're moving fast, but that doesn't mean we're going anywhere past second base on this London trip.

The flight starts off a little rocky. Literally. As I confessed to Dalton, I am terrified of flying. But first of all, I'm a firm believer in facing my fears, and also, if I didn't fly, how would I ever get anywhere? Long car trips make me a little queasy, and don't even get me started on trains. Nonetheless, flying always freaks me out more at first—so we're on the runway and the plane starts making those really aggressive *vrooommmm* sounds beneath our seats, and I grab Dalton's arm. His incredibly cool, calm, and collected arm.

"It's the sound," I explain. I'm gripping hard, I can't help it.

"That?" He laughs. "That's just the engine, love. Getting ready to take off."

I gulp audibly. "Take off from the ground? Already?"

"Yes, already. Are you all right?" He holds my hand and looks into my eyes, probably trying to find a sign of the somewhat sane person he invited on this trip. Before I have time to respond, the plane begins racing forward and I can feel my face drain of color. I'm pale as a ghost as the plane lifts off the tarmac and goes teetering into the air.

"Are you all right?" he asks again.

"Uh-huh. I'm just . . . um . . . is this normal?"

"For an airplane to be in the air? Yes. Otherwise they'd call it a groundplane."

"Ha, no, I mean is it normal for it to be doing that shaking thing?" As I say this, the plane's light quivering becomes full-on quaking. Fall-out-of-the-sky-level quaking. "Oh god, are we going to die? I don't want to die, I don't want to die." I swear my life is flashing before my eyes and all I can think is what a bitch I was to Ellie and how I'll never get a chance to say I'm sorry.

"Babe," Dalton says, half worried (for my sanity), half amused (quirky is cute, right? RIGHT?), "it's just some turbulence. This happens. It's normal."

"Is it really? Do you promise?"

"Yes. I promise. Look." He directs my attention at the flight attendants, who are casually examining one another's manicures at the front of the plane. "Do they seem worried? They do these flights literally every day, so if something was wrong, they would know about it."

"Okay, I guess that makes sense. So as long as the flight attendants look calm, there's nothing to worry about?"

"Exactly."

"But what if they're not paying attention?"

"What? Not paying attention?" My God, he must feel like he's talking to a preschooler. "They're completely plugged in at all times to any information the captain has. They'd know if something was wrong, trust me. And besides, there's literally nothing to be concerned about. Even if something did go wrong, these plans have a million backup systems."

"Really?"

"What is this, your first time on a plane?"

"No! I actually have to fly all the time for meet and greets, promotional things, whatever. I just can't ever get used to it. Probably never will."

"Boy, are you adorable," he says, poking the tip of my nose. "Now calm down and relax. Order a movie and get comfortable. We have a long flight ahead of us."

"All right." I sigh deeply. "I'll try to relax. What movie are you gonna watch?"

"Oh, I'm not going to watch a movie. I have to use these flights to catch up on my sleep. I got that tip from Kim and Kanye."

Ah, the *other* jet-setting power couple.

Two hours into the flight and I've tried everything I possibly can to relax. I've anxiously scrolled through all the movies that Virgin has to offer (they all seem too scary or too cheesy or too serious). I've ordered almost everything off the snack menu (Chips Ahoy!, Pringles, Gummy Bears, chocolate-covered pretzels, you name it). I've unpacked and repacked my travel bag. I've written a list of things I want to see in London (all I have written on it is Big Ben, because I don't actually know what else there is to see over there). I've curled my body up into a ball and tried counting sheep (all efforts to fall asleep were in vain). I've tried listening to soothing music (Mojave 3, Iron & Wine, even some Enya). I've tried looking out the window (bad idea, we are *way* too high up). Last but not least, I've chewed on some melatonin gummies to knock me out. None of this is working, and all the while Dalton is passed out with his earplugs in and his tongue hanging halfway out of his mouth. Charming. He somehow manages to even sleep through the most violent patches of turbulence. It's. So. Frustrating.

The thing is, I know why I can't make myself relax, and it has to do with more than just being thirty thousand miles in the air with no control over the situation whatsoever. It's about Ellie. I can't stop thinking about what Dalton said, about how if @ThatBitchHarper really was her, the last thing she'd do is tweet about Jamba Juice. Why give herself away so easily? There's only one answer, and that is, *she didn't. It's not Ellie*. It makes much more sense for it to be someone who wants me to think it was her. But who could that be? I try to think of who else could have known we were at Jamba Juice. Someone who just happened to see us on the street walking in? But what are the chances that the person who knew about my first date with Dalton just happened to see Ellie and me walk into Jamba Juice? Seems insanely unlikely. Unless @ThatBitchHarper has been following me. Could that be possible?

I take out a pen and paper and decide I'll use the next seven hours to get to the bottom of this:

Suspects

People who knew Dalton asked me out:

- Ellie
- Someone who overheard at Chateau Marmont?
- Dalton
- Someone Dalton told?
- Someone Ellie told?

People who knew I went on a date with Dalton:

- Ellie
- Dalton

- My mom
- Jack
- The British girls from Moonshadows
- Any number of people at Moonshadows
- The paparazzi —>anyone who has seen their pictures
- Any number of people at the Magic Castle
- Dalton's jerk friends

People who knew I was at Jamba Juice:

- Ellie
- Anyone on the street who saw us go in
- The Jamba Juice cashier

People who don't like me:

- Dalton's jerk friend Roger
- Ashley Adler
- Ashley's blond squad
- Maybe Jack? (if he resents me for rejecting him?)
- Maybe Ellie (if she's secretly jealous and resents my success?)

I try to pinpoint where there's crossover. I figure if I can find someone who fits into all four categories, they have to be the guilty party. But as far as I can tell, there's nobody. I stare at the lists until all the names start to blur together, and before I know it, I'm finally, blissfully asleep.

CHAPTER 9

Forty-Eight Hours in London

So have you ever seen *The Parent Trap*? The 1998 one, I mean, with little Lindsay Lohan when she was just about the cutest kid ever and legitimately so crazy talented. There's that scene where Hallie Parker (the scrappier of the twins) shows up in London for the first time as her twin sister, Annie (the posh one), and she takes in the sights as her cab drives through the town that is so magically foreign to her Californian eyes, and she's just so excited that she rests her arms on the window ledge and sticks her head out like a dog. That's how I always imagined it would be like when I first arrived in London, but it isn't.

It is SO MUCH BETTER.

After we get off the plane, slog through customs, and pick up our luggage, we hop into the private car waiting for Dalton and drive through residential neighborhoods so quaint and quintessentially British that they look like they have been cut straight out of Peter Pan, past parks as big and lush as forests, past Buckingham

Palace, which is, hello, where the QUEEN lives. The *queen.* We drive in a roundabout around the Royal Albert Hall (where the Spice Girls perform at the end of *Spice World,* duh), and zigzag across roads that are about ten times more exciting than the ones in America; they're all windy and narrow and unpredictable, so that the whole trip to our hotel feels like Disneyland's Mr. Toad's Wild Ride. Hashtag best ride ever. I seriously cannot believe how delightful and charming this town is. Never in my life have I seen anything so picturesque; I've apparently flown out of Los Angeles and straight into a storybook. Luckily, I think to pull out my phone and record almost all of this amazingness. I can't speak for my followers, but *I* will want to remember this forever.

The Kensington Hotel at 113 Queen's Gate is to die for. There's a gold-plated fireplace in the lobby and bowls upon bowls of crisp red apples. My eyes dart around like I'm a kid in a candy shop. The suite itself is on the tenth floor, decorated with lush satins and spiraling gold accents and Victorian-era patterned carpets. The walls are painted deep, steel blue with white trim, and there's a grand piano placed casually by the window. Oh, and get this, the slate-tiled bathroom floor is heated so your feet don't have to be cold during middle-of-the-night visits, of which for me there are many (I drink a lot of water).

Now, I have seen some nice things in my short time on this earth, but nothing as nice as Dalton James's suite at the Kensington Hotel (with two bedrooms, *thank you very much!* The guy really is a gentleman, as it turns out). We order room service right away (it's breakfast time, but I'm eight hours behind and can't tell if I'm hungry or nauseous or tired or dead)—ice cream parfaits, hash browns, orange juice—and consume it all in a daze.

"Are you ready?" he asks, finishing off a champagne flute and standing up.

"Ready for what?"

"To see the town, of course. You didn't think we flew all the way to England just to have room service in a five-star hotel, did you? We can do that in Los Angeles anytime."

"Oh, but I'm far too fancy and important to leave my hotel room." I dramatically put the back of my hand to my forehead and fake the best British accent I can. "Can't I just lounge in bed eating tea and crumpets all day?"

"Very funny. Your accent is wretched."

"I know it is, darling," I tease, and then switch back to my normal American voice. "I'm just kidding. Of course I'm ready to go out on the town. I was born ready."

"That's my girl," he says and opens his arms to me. I jump into them and he holds me up successfully for one spectacular moment before losing his balance and falling, Harper and all, onto the fancy-as-hell carpet.

Our forty-eight hours in London are a whirlwind of romance and adventure. Ugh, I know that *sounds* corny, but trust me, it was anything but. On the first day we zip around the town using the Tube, wearing baseball hats and sunglasses so as to stay under the radar (eeeh, so glamorous!). He takes me to Portobello Road to see where they filmed *Notting Hill*, then to the Tower of London to see where Henry the Eighth cut off all his wives' heads, then to the Tate Modern to see my favorite paintings (Picasso! Van Gogh! Rothko!), then to the Ritz for tea and cucumber sandwiches, then to Leicester Square to see a production of *Billy Elliot*, then to central London, where we take a moonlit boat ride down the river Thames and kiss under the stars while the boat conductor points out historical landmarks along the shore. Afterward we take the Tube to Shoreditch (the Silver Lake of London; in other words, the hipster part of town) to see some punk band that some of Dalton's childhood "mates" are in. His mates in London are a lot nicer and less pretentious than his friends in Los Angeles, that's for sure. After the show we all go out to a hilariously stereotypical British pub (Union Jacks everywhere, the oily smell of fish and chips heavy in the air), where they drink whiskey like it's water and I charm everyone with my surprisingly impressive pool skills.

"What are you doing dating this wanker?" one friend named Alfie asks, jabbing Dalton in his rib cage. "Don't you know you're far too pretty and clever for a guy like him?" Alfie has shaggy black hair and gigantic holes in his earlobes.

"Oh, I think he's all right," I say, winking at Dalton.

"Are you trying to steal my girlfriend, mate?" Dalton grips Alfie's shoulder, pretending to get all macho and protective. "Huh? Are ya?"

"No way, man. If she's too good for you, she's way too good for me."

I giggle. Oh, Alfie, why can't more men be like you?

Hanging out with Dalton's childhood buddies is the most fun I've had in a while. It feels so refreshing to see him being treated like an old friend, not an Internet star, but an actual human being. And from what I can tell, it's refreshing for him too; he seems lighter and more at ease in England, his shoulders looser and his entire face softened.

By the time we've finished our third game of pool (and I've won them all, thank you very much), it's almost three in the morning. The Tube has closed down long ago, so Dalton calls a car to take us back to the hotel.

"Did you have a fun day?" he asks as we slip inside the monstrous suite, unbuttoning my coat for me and dimming the lights with a switch behind my head.

"Ummm, is the pope Catholic?"

"I don't know. Should we give him a call to find out?"

"I think the pope *probably* has better things to do than take our phone calls."

He rests his forehead against my forehead. "Hey, *we* are very important people."

"You are, at least," I say.

"Me? No. Compared to you I'm barely significant."

"Oh, please."

"No, really. If you weren't an extremely important person, would I do this?" He scoops me up off the floor and holds me like a newlywed bride, then spins me around and swings me gently onto the bed.

"Voilà," he says, "treatment fit for a princess. Which you are. To me."

"Stop it . . ." I trail off in a tone of voice that actually says, "Keep going. Forever." He unbuckles my boots and slips them off my feet one by one.

"You know, I'm surprised your parents let you sleep in a foreign country in a room alone with some strange guy they've never met."

"Well, they trust me. And I trust you."

"As you should." He clicks on the TV and the red Netflix logo pops onto the screen. "My intentions are pure."

"Oh, really? Because it seems to me that your intentions are to Netflix and chill, if you know what I mean."

"My intentions are Netflix and giving you a foot massage, thank you very much."

"Fine by me. But that's all you're going to get."

"Me? That's all *you're* going to get."

We both laugh and he massages my feet, sore from walking all day, while *The Prince and Me* with Julia Stiles plays in the background. My eyelids begin to grow heavy, and within minutes I can feel myself drifting off to sleep, more peaceful than I've ever been.

In the morning he takes me to Hyde Park and we sit by a pond watching ducks paddle through the water, hunting down bread crumbs. The whole thing is so charming I could explode. We just sit there peacefully, in silence, holding hands, basking in each other's presence. That's the best part: in such a short time I've

gone from nervous fangirl to totally comfortable around him. The more I act like my truest self, the more he seems to fall for me, so why bother being anything other than 100 percent me?

"I wish you didn't have to go home today," he says.

"Me too."

"Stay with me the rest of the week," he says impulsively. "And then come with me to New York next weekend."

"What's in New York?"

"I have to do Jimmy Fallon."

"You have to *do* Jimmy Fallon?"

"I have to appear on his show. Promote the next *Sacred* movie."

"Seriously? Ugh, I would love to come with you, but my flight back to L.A. is in three hours and my parents will literally murder me if I'm not on it."

"I know, I know. Is it so wrong that I want you to be with me all the time?"

"Are you kidding? It's not wrong, it's the best thing I've ever heard."

"If I could, I would shrink you down and take you with me in my pocket wherever I go."

"Okay, now that's the best thing I've ever heard. I'm all for that as long as your pocket fabric is soft. I'm thinking satin, maybe?"

"It's settled, then. I'll get satin lining for all my pockets."

A few hours later Dalton and his driver drop me at Heathrow and he kisses me goodbye, murmuring how much he'll miss me. I wave at him until he's out of sight and then go through the usual airport rigmarole, eventually boarding the plane and settling into my first-class seat. This time I'm not afraid to fly. In fact, I don't feel afraid of anything anymore. *Life is too sweet for fear*, I think, resting my head against the plush leather chair. I close my eyes, and before I know it, I've slept my way safely back to Los Angeles.

TUTORIAL #6

Five Insanely Easy Back-to-School Hairstyles

Hi, guys! So, after almost three whole days of forgetting school is even a thing, I am being forced to return. *Cringes* The only thing I can think of to cheer me up and get me through this upcoming week is to cook up some back-to-school hairstyles and pair them with my favorite outfits! I gotta keep up with the trends, my friends.

1. Okay, so I'm going to start off style number one by curling my hair, just because I think it looks better to have styles with nicely textured, wavy hair. So I'm just brushing out my hair and making a middle part, and then I'm using my NuMe Lustrum set. I've been using their curling wands for literally like three years, no joke; they last forever, and there are like five different barrels in the set, which is crazy. I'm going to use the biggest one, because like I said, I really want big-textured hair. So then you're just going to go ahead and curl your whole head of hair, I'm sure you know how to do that by now, and if you don't, you can see I'm taking one-inch sections and wrapping it around for about ten seconds. Lastly, I'm using some argan oil to smooth it out and prevent frizz. Voilà! Once your hair is completely curled, it's time to move on to the rest of the hairstyle. For this one, I'm just using this really adorable, girlie-looking headband (any headband that is beaded and super skinny will do!) and pulling out the front pieces of my

hair so that they hang loose in front of the headband. In my opinion, this makes all the difference, so much better than if it were all slicked back into the headband. To go with this hairstyle I'm wearing a pink printed sundress with flat white strappy leather sandals for a beachy, almost earthy kind of vibe.

2. This next hairstyle is probably the easiest thing ever, and we all know how to do it! It's just some simple low-hanging pigtails. I'm bringing it back, you guys. I feel like I'm five, but I'm loving it. So I'll start by just dividing my hair into two sections and securing them with elastic hair ties, then putting a floppy hat on top for some extra fierceness. As for the rest of my outfit, I'm going to wear an orangy, mustard-colored crop top with some flared jeans (yes, I said flared). I just feel really seventies in this outfit, so why not go all the way?
3. Hairstyle number three is a half-up, half-down kind of thing and it's almost festivally with the braids. All I'm doing is taking a two-inch section from either side of my head and braiding each one normally (or you can fishtail if you have those fancy skillz), then wrapping them around and crossing them at the back of my head (great for hiding areas that have had to have gum cut out of them, BTW) and securing with a few bobby pins. No big deal. Like with hairstyle #1, I'm going to leave some pieces out loose in the front for an extra whimsical look. To go along with this look I'm wearing a really cute white romper with a crème-colored knitted cardigan. You got this.
4. Next is the sporty look, I guess, if you wanna call it that. I'm going to start this by parting my hair in a dramatic side part. You can pick the side you want to do, but I'm going with the left, meaning

most of my hair is flipped over to the left side of my head. Then I'm making two small sections of hair on the right side of my head and basically just braiding them normally, kind of like cornrows except I'm really not talented enough to do real cornrows. It doesn't matter, they can be regular old "boring" braids, just make them as tight as possible for this look. You can have your hair wavy or curly or straight for this one, whatever you want. For this outfit I'm gonna throw on a really casual sweater, casual white shorts and some basic slip-on shoes. Nothin' fancy, just super comfy!

5. The last hairstyle I'm preparing for this week is perfect if you're anything like me and you hate having your hair in your face. It just bugs me, I hate it, always gotta pull it behind my ears. Ugh. So all you have to do is have a side part and then just start twisting your hair from the top to the bottom on both sides, and then secure them together with an elastic band in a side ponytail. And that's pretty much it. Your hair is now out of your face, but it's still down and wavy and cute all at the same time. For this outfit I'm wearing a black crop top that has a white stripe on the neckline, a brown suede skirt, and some black sneakers!

So, if you're ever dreading going back to school, try using these five styles to keep your spirits up. Sometimes when you look amazing, your mood follows suit!

You are my everything goals.

Lots of love, Harper

CHAPTER 10

Miss Harper of the People

The first day back in school after any amount of freedom, however brief, is always a difficult transition, but today feels extra harsh, extra jarring. Maybe it's because (A) I got such a sweet taste of independence and adventure that school now seems extra dull and oppressive in comparison. Or maybe it's because (B) after my trip to London I'm no closer to knowing who @ThatBitchHarper really is, nor have I successfully made amends to Ellie for my horrible accusation. Or maybe it's because (C) sitting in Ms. Bulow's first-period English class waiting for the bell to ring, I'm surrounded by a flurry of sixteen-year-olds sharing and comparing their PSAT scores with irritating levels of enthusiasm and concern in their voices. The answer is (D) all of the above.

The PSATs—that's Preliminary SATs, as in preparation for the SATs, as in a test you take over and over again starting two years before the actual SATs so that you can be PREPARED for them. As if studying all of high school isn't going to be enough to prepare you. One thing I've never understood: if the SATs are supposed to measure how prepared you are for college, and high school is supposed to prepare you for college, then why isn't it enough to just pay attention during high school in order to do well on the SATs? Why aren't our actual high school classes teaching us everything we need to know in order to do well on these wacky exams? Why, during sophomore year, do I have to start taking an extra class just to get me ready for one test that all my other classes are supposed to be preparing me for?! I don't know much about conspiracies, TBQH, but this most certainly sounds like one to me.

Now, IMHO I have better things to do than figure out what or who is behind this conspiracy, let alone what the sinister motives are, but I'm pretty sure I don't want to go to college and get stuck in a cycle of test taking (life is too short for that stress), so this is the first year I've said "hard pass" to the PSATs.

Ashley Adler leans over my shoulder, her voice all fake and spun-sugar sweet. "Hey, Harper, your hair is looking a little . . . choppy. Having a bad hair day?" Um, one question: why is this bitch always sitting behind me?

"More like a bad hair life." Gigi O'Neil, her wing girl with eyelash extensions and too much lip liner, snickers.

"Thanks for your heartfelt concern," I say without turning around to face her, "but I'm fine."

"I don't know about that," Ashley continues. "You didn't look fine in *People* mag leaving Moonshadows with Dalton James. I mean, did you think those ribbons covered up the massive chunk of hair missing from the back of your head? So weird, you'd think an Internet celeb such as yourself could afford a professional to effectively cover that thing up. I guess you're not all that important after all."

I don't respond, easily seeing through to her scalding jealousy. She's never been in a tabloid, she's never dated a celebrity. Hell, she's never really dated anyone, probably because she is genuinely NOT A NICE PERSON. Could she be responsible for @ThatBitchHarper? She definitely has the tone down to a tee.

"So what's your score?" Gigi continues to prod.

"I don't have one," I say without turning around to face her.

"What? Everyone has one." Ashley is beaming; I can practically hear it from behind me. "You can tell us, Harper, no need to be ashamed of a low score."

"I don't have a score," I say again, turning around this time, "because I didn't take the test."

"Wait, are you serious? That's ridiculous."

"Why? The PSATs just aren't in my lane. I'm following my success and my dreams, all right? The SATs are supposed to reflect college preparedness. When I take them next year they'll reflect exactly how much high school has prepared me for college. Training myself until I'm able to get higher and higher scores doesn't make sense to me. I am what I am."

"Well, as self-loving and inspirational as that sounds, it's pretty naive. If you get a low score, you won't get accepted into any good schools."

"Yeah," adds Gigi, "you'll have to go to, like, a state school." She shudders, sticking her tongue out in disgust.

"First of all, what's wrong with a state school? I mean, so what?"

The girls share a glance that seems to say *Aww, poor Harper.*

"Harper," Ashley begins to explain with a tone of exaggerated patience, "anyone can get into a state school. When you graduate college, no one will hire you because they'll think you're just a loser like everyone else. If you go to a state school, you won't be special."

"There aren't enough hours in a day for me to even begin explaining how twisted and classist that logic is."

"Oooh, twisted *and* classist. Miss Harper of the people. You're so fake, Harper. We all know you're just going to use Dalton's fame to get into some Ivy League you aren't smart enough to go to." Ashley turns away, apparently finished with the conversation, and she and Gigi begin conferring about which top schools they're already both thinking of applying to.

I could use my own *fame to get into an Ivy League,* I think to myself, but am not proud of it.

"Do you not have anything better to do than pick on me?" I try to block her out.

"Too bad the whole world knows about your drug problem now. Probably couldn't get into college at this point even if you wanted to. No one's going to accept a crackhead, now are they?"

"What are you talking about?" I spin around in my seat. Now she has my full attention.

"I'm talking about @ThatBitchHarper. Haven't you read her latest tweet?"

"Her *latest—*"

"*YouTube 'star' Harper Ambrose isn't so perfect after all.*" Ashley's reading off her phone loudly to anyone who is listening. People start leaning in to hear better. "*She's failing high school and inside sources say it's all because her addiction to crack cocaine.* Then there's a frowny face emoji." She gives me a very triumphant, practically evil stare. Murmurs run through the room.

"*Crack*?" I can't believe it. "Why on earth would I ever in a million years do crack? Where would I even get crack?"

"I dunno." She shrugs, "You tell me."

"I'm not addicted to crack. I've never tried crack or come close to trying it. No, you know what, this is fine, nobody's going to believe her."

"I believe her," says Ashley.

"Me too," says Gigi.

"Sorry, let me rephrase that. Nobody who *matters* is going to believe her."

"Oh, I don't know about that. A bunch of people are responding and it doesn't look good."

I grab my phone and open Twitter. I have to see this for myself.

Sure enough, my so-called fans are tweeting back at @ThatBitchHarper.

@Harpernator12: @ThatBitchHarper, can't believe I used to look up to a crack head! RIP role model!

@Nmbr1HarperFan: @ThatBitchHarper Feel so betrayed. SMH.

@HarperGoals: @ThatBitchHarper So gross. Doesn't she know she's going to lose her teeth? Didn't realize she was dumb ☹ #disappointed.

Um, what the HELL is happening right now? How could people who call themselves my fans possibly believe this made-up piece of gossip? Clearly I overestimated the loyalty of my followers. This is awful. What if this rumor spreads and everyone believes it and I start actually losing followers? What if it actually means I can't go to college? Sure, I don't know if I want to, but I'm not ready to give it up as an option! @ThatBitchHarper has officially gone from a nuisance to an actual threat. Now she's crossed the line.

After class I'm determined to get the hell out of there, devising a plan to never see Ashley or any of her deranged groupies ever again, but Mrs. Bulow stops me at the door.

"Harper, could you stay a moment?"

"Erm . . . I kinda have to get to second period."

"I'll write you a pass."

"Oh, uh . . . okay." What could this possibly be about? Teachers never want to talk to me: I get good grades and I stay out of trouble. I'm an expert at staying under the radar.

"I heard what Ashley and Gigi were saying to you," she says sympathetically. Mrs. Bulow is a prim and proper lady. She wears her graying blond hair in a tight bun and a bronze brooch on her lapel.

"Oh, yeah, that," I say. "You don't have to worry about that, I can handle those girls. It's no big deal."

She smiles. "I'm sure you can, but here's the thing. I know they're mean girls and trying to hurt your feelings, but the fact of the matter is, they're right. When it comes to college and the SATs, that is. You're a smart girl, and believe me when I say you deserve an education of value and substance. At a state school or a . . . community college"—she speaks these words as if it's painful to have them in her mouth—"you won't be intellectually stimulated. Those students don't take learning seriously, and it will be way too easy for you to fall into a hole of parties and boys."

"Okay, but—"

"Before you say you know what you want, let me just give you something. One moment." She turns to her desk, takes out a stack of ultra-collegiate-looking folders, and hands them to me. Smith, Wellesley, and Sarah Lawrence.

"I know, I know, all-girls schools probably aren't the most appealing of options, especially for someone like you—"

"Wait, why for someone like me?"

"Well, you're very focused on your appearance, hair, and makeup and clothes are the center of your life. Aren't they? That's what that channel thing you film is all about . . . the BooTube? WhoTube?"

"YouTube," I correct her through gritted teeth, barely keeping my temper in check.

Mrs. Bulow nods encouragingly, as if she didn't just basically call me shallow and say something wildly insulting. "Exactly. And who can blame you? You're sixteen and you've already made a career off these things, the art of being attractive to the opposite sex. I hear the students chattering, I know your success has led to some fame. So why would you want to go to college? Especially an all-girls college, where there are no boys to appreciate all the effort you put into your appearance? But what I'm trying to say is, I think it would be really good for you to be in an environment where appearances don't matter and you can really focus on your studies and on bettering yourself as a human being from the inside. Does any of what I'm saying make sense to you?"

Mrs. Bulow's words feel like a slap in the face. I know she didn't intend to be hurtful, but she was. ICYMI (in case you missed it), Mrs. Bulow just implied that I am boy crazy and vain, and that if I continue on this path of boy craziness and vanity without going to college (God forbid), things won't turn out so well for me. Nobody, and I mean NOBODY, understands me at this stupid school.

"With all due respect, Mrs. Bulow," I say, looking up from the university information folders, "you've got me all wrong."

"Oh?" She sounds as though she doesn't actually care to hear what I have to say—it doesn't matter to her, she thinks she already has me all figured out—but I keep going anyway.

"Yes, I like boys. I do. But my hair and clothes and makeup—none of this is for them, it's for me. It's my method of self-expression; it's how I create a safe place for myself. And my videos aren't designed to help girls get the guy, they're designed to help girls to feel beautiful in their own skin regardless of what boys or even the other girls at school think. And sure, maybe I'd like a college education—I do love learning, I really do—but I don't like it when other people, people who don't know me, think it's what I *need*. How is telling girls they need a college education any better than telling girls they need a husband? If you ask me, it's just another way to tell us who to be and what to do, instead of letting us discover who we are for ourselves. Thank you for these, I'll look them over, but for now I have to get to class."

I turn on my heel without another word and head down the hallway of the language building, feeling high off a major adrenaline rush. Whoa. Where did those words even come from? From my soul, that's where. I'm feeling empowered, I'm feeling strong. What I said was true. I don't need college any more than I need a man, and I can't let society—I *won't* let society—tell me who to be or how to live my life. And what's more, I won't let anyone make me feel bad about who I am or the choices I make.

The school day ends with me feeling refreshed and renewed. It feels amazing to realize that I actually like myself and the person I'm growing into, even if that person doesn't end up going to college or pleasing the high school administration. Surely I'm on this planet for reasons other than to do what other people want me to do, and as I walk out to my car I'm thrilled by this new realization. Aaanndd that's when things take a bit of a turn.

My car won't start. As it turns out, I left all my lights on while I was in school for six hours, and now the battery is dead. Why, universe, why? What are you trying to tell me?! I close my eyes and grip the steering wheel as if praying for an answer, but none comes. Maybe because I'm not so much praying as I am repeating, "Ughhhhhhh, so annoyyinggg," over and over in my head.

I can't call my mom or dad. They're both at work and have explicitly said to stop interrupting their workdays with this type of thing (I'd be lying if I said it's never happened before).

"Use your Triple A card next time, sweetie," Mom had said. "That's what it's for."

But I don't want to call stupid Triple A, I want to call Ellie. With a heavy dose of nostalgia, I remember the time her car died at my house the morning after a Mumford & Sons show at the Palladium. My parents weren't home and we took it upon ourselves to try to jump-start her car using the cables I had in my trunk. We didn't know anything about cables or engines and the whole thing was an epic fail, but we laughed our way through it. Then it had started raining and we had no choice but to laugh even harder. I wish more than anything in that moment that I could call Ellie and she'd forgive me and we could try to work this one out together, like old times. I pick up my phone and start to dial her number but then think better of it. *This isn't the time,* I thought. *I would hate for her to think I was reaching out only because I wanted help. I need my apology to be pure so that she knows how sorry I really am.*

Reluctantly, I call AAA, but they won't be able to get to me for an hour. Of course, just my luck. Just then a black Jeep pulls up next to mine, and who might it be? None other than Jack Walsh.

He motions for me to roll down my window, which I can't do, because my car is dead, so I open my door instead.

"Hey, you all right?" he asks, reading my face, which is no doubt disgruntled by this point. Why does he have a habit of turning up when I'm a hot mess?

"My car won't start."

"Sometimes you have the worst luck." He smiles kindly, sympathetically.

"Yeah," I say, "sometimes."

"I'd offer you a ride, but you probably just wanna call AAA."

"I just called them, actually. They'll be here in an hour."

"An hour? That seems like a long time for them."

"That's what they said." I shrug.

"Well, I think I already know your general attitude on the subject, but I'm gonna ask anyway: are you in the mood for Ben & Jerry's? Just something to do until Triple A gets here?"

"You know what?" I think about it for a moment, and then decide. "I'd love some ice cream right about now."

Ben & Jerry's is and always has been one of my very favorite places. The cool air-conditioning, the paintings of cows grazing on grass, the quirky little drawings on the tables all about the company's illustrious history, and best of all, the smell of rainbow sprinkles and baked waffle cones that permeates literally everything in the parlor. Parlor, is that the right word? What qualifies a place as a parlor? Is serving ice cream enough, or does it need to be all fancy and old-fashioned? Maybe I have it all wrong, maybe a parlor is something else entirely. *Hmmm . . .*

This is the road my mind is wandering down when Jack interrupts my thoughts. "Mint chocolate cookie with rainbow sprinkles in a rainbow-sprinkled cone?" he asks me point-blank.

"What?" I look at him, baffled, as if he's speaking some foreign language.

He laughs. "Mint chocolate cookie with rainbow sprinkles in a rainbow-sprinkled cone," he repeats. "Is that still your Ben & Jerry's order of choice?"

"Yes! How could you possibly remember that?" I can't help it, I'm equal parts stunned and delighted.

"How could I possibly *not* remember that? You always got the exact same thing whenever you, Gwen, and I went out for ice cream together. It was always one of my favorite things about you."

"But you . . ." I search for the right words, but suddenly my brain feels scrambled and fuzzy. "You didn't even notice me."

"I did, though. I thought you knew that." His eyes are inscrutable as his gaze meets mine, and I don't entirely dislike the way this makes me feel. Which in and of itself is disarming.

"Next?" The woman up at the counter asks for our order.

"One mint chocolate cookie with rainbow sprinkles in a rainbow-sprinkled cone." Jack takes the initiative, ordering for me. "And one fudge sundae in a cup, please." He looks back and smiles at me. "And you know what? Go ahead and throw some rainbow sprinkles on there too."

Oh no. Feelings. Happening. Warm. Fluttery. Must. Stop. Feelings. Must. Stop. Warm. Fluttery. Feelings. From. Happening. For almost two whole years I've kept my crush on Jack at bay, but now, standing here in one of the sweetest, most sugary rooms on earth, it's all flooding back. *Well, it's too late, Jack,* I say to him, except silently and only in my head, *you had your chance and you blew it.* I'm with Dalton now, and he treats me right, so there. This train has sailed. What? No, this ship has sailed. This train has left the station? *You have to get out of here,* I tell myself, *get out while you still can.*

"Oh, hey, you know what?" I look down at my phone. "Triple A is almost at my car. I'm gonna head back."

"Wait, I'll take you."

"No, no, it's okay, really. I'm just going to . . . run."

"You're going to run all the way back to campus?"

"Yes. I'm sorry, have my ice cream for me, and I promise I'll pay you back at school tomorrow. Promise." I sprint out the door and run a few blocks, then stop to catch my breath. My heart is pounding. Why did I have to literally run? The sun beats down on me and one thing becomes crystal clear: I am a hot mess.

Before I can even try to begin to understand what just happened in there with Jack, my phone vibrates. It's a Twitter notification. Not just any Twitter notification, it's from @ThatBitchHarper. Goddammit, this is the last thing I need right now.

@ThatBitchHarper: Spotted: Harper riding in cars with boys, PLURAL. Turns out this wannabe celeb wants to have her rainbow-sprinkled ice cream cone and eat it too. Maybe @DaltonJamesOfficial isn't the only player in this "relationship."

Attached are two pictures. One is of me in Jack's car, and from the angle it's taken at, we look like we're kissing. Which of course we weren't. Curse you, optical illusions. The second one is of us walking into Ben & Jerry's. Dammit. Who could possibly have taken this?

Just then my phone vibrates with another tweet. It's a follow-up:

@ThatBitchHarper: Better watch your back, Harper. I have eyes everywhere.

Oh my goodness. A new set of feelings rolls in. I'm now a confusing combination of infuriated and relieved. Why? I now know exactly who @ThatBitchHarper is.

As soon as Triple A has finished jump-starting my car and leaves me with a stern warning to turn my lights off next time, I drive like a woman possessed out to the Pacific Coast Highway, convertible top down and sunglasses on. Like a warrior.

The PCH is long and winding, it feels like it goes on forever, the ocean glittering to my left as I drive past Santa Monica Canyon, Pacific Palisades, Temescal Canyon, Topanga Canyon, all the way to Malibu. Once in Malibu, I have to drive inland almost two miles, up a steep road even more curvy and coiled than the PCH, which now looks like nothing more than a thin line down below. As I drive, I replay every tweet over and over in my mind, wondering how it took me this long to connect all the dots. The personal vendetta quality of the tweets, the way this troll knew so much about me, the bitter, holier-than-thou tone that permeated every word she wrote—it finally all made sense: @ThatBitchHarper could really only be one person, so why hadn't I seen this before?

I arrive at a gated community at the top of the hill, where I'm faced with a silvery keypad. I used to spend so many weekends here, so many sleepovers and birthday parties and just regular old Tuesdays. I search my memory for the pass code and am surprised when it comes to me as easily as it does: *799429#

To my absolute shock, the code works. *I can't believe they never changed it,* I think. After a low beep, the iron gate slides open and I drive in, park in front of the biggest of the Spanish Colonial Revival mansions, and ring the doorbell.

The woman who comes to the door is very pretty and looks almost exactly like her daughter, albeit twenty-seven years older.

"Harper?" She stares in disbelief.

"Hi, Mrs. Crane," I say. "Is Gwen home?"

CHAPTER 11

Second-Rate Gossip Girl

Gwen comes to the door in Victoria's Secret pajamas; pink drawstring shorts and a gray tank top that shows off her perfectly flat stomach. She's gotten a lot taller since the last time I saw her; her hair is much more blond and there's a lot more of it, cascading effortlessly all around her shoulders. She never did have to try very hard to look incredible.

"Harper. What are you doing here? Are you insane?" she asks.

"I'll leave you two alone to talk," Mrs. Crane says, then slinks away.

"Am *I* insane?" I try to keep my voice as low and calm as possible, but it's a challenge. "You're running a Twitter account designed to sabotage my life!"

Panic flashes across her face, but she shakes it off and smirks. "Oh, don't be so dramatic."

"It took me a while to figure out it was you, Gwen, because quite frankly I had more or less forgotten about you. For a second there you actually had me believing it was Ellie, after that Jamba Juice tweet. I was furious with her, never thinking to consider who resents me the most: you."

"How'd you figure out it was me?" She sighs deeply and crosses her arms in defeat.

"You tweeted that I'm a wannabe celeb. That's what you called me on the last day we spoke. Before middle school graduation. And then you called out my rainbow sprinkle cone preference—that gave you away. Nobody else besides you and Jack know that. And I was with Jack. That leaves you. Then it all came back to me, how we used to binge-watch *Pretty Little Liars* and pretend to be Aria and Hanna. That last tweet made it clear, your Twitter account was an attempt at being A. You wanted to haunt me the way A taunts the girls in *Pretty Little Liars*. A calls the girls 'bitches.' That's why you call me That Bitch Harper. You've been a wannabe A all along."

"Ouch," Gwen quips sarcastically.

"So why, Gwen? Why do you hate me so much? Just because I had a crush on your boyfriend and kept it a secret? Would you have honestly preferred that I told you? I wasn't trying to steal him from you, I was trying to make my feelings go away so that I could be a good friend to you!"

"That's not what it's about. That's not why I hate you."

"Okay, then why?"

"You really want to know the truth?"

"Please."

"Ugh, you're just a fake nobody and you ruined my life! *Okay?*"

"What do you mean, I ruined your life? How?"

She looks up to the ceiling as if trying not to cry. "You don't understand. You took everything from me and never had to pay for it. You got famous overnight and I got nothing. I was supposed to be famous, I'm the talented actress. You're just some nerdy girl who knows stuff about makeup and has too much free time on her hands."

"I still don't see how I ruined your life. I don't get it. All I did was—"

"Wait, do you still not know?" She stares, tears practically drying up on the spot.

"Not know what?"

"Are you serious? You must know by now."

"No! I don't. What don't I know?"

"The day before I looked through your diary, Jack told me he couldn't be with me anymore. Because he was in love with someone else. You."

What. Is. Happening.

I stare at Gwen for a moment, openmouthed and totally confused. "That's not possible. He was in love with you. He was obsessed with you. Remember?"

"That's what I thought. But it was a lie. He was just dating me because he thought you'd never like him like that. And I liked him, so he settled for me. Even though it was you he wanted all along."

"But . . . but . . ." I stammer, "but he told me he just wanted to be friends."

"Yeah, I told him if he ever acted on his feelings for you, I'd post a video I have of him falling off his skateboard and crying. Trust me, it's humiliating."

"You're insane!" I can't believe what I'm hearing. "But wait, you're telling me he actually liked me even when he said he liked you?"

"Yup."

"But . . . but . . ." I stammer again, "you're so much prettier than I am."

Gwen nods solemnly. "I agree," she says, "that's part of why it's so weird. But I guess Jack has a different opinion. Or maybe looks don't matter to him or something, I don't know. Anyways, Jack had broken up with me the day before I found your stupid diary, but I wasn't telling people yet because I knew it would just be a matter of time before he came to his senses and asked to get back together. But then I saw all that sad, sad stuff you had written about him and I knew . . . I knew you wanted him too, and that meant I would never get him back."

"So you decided to get revenge with a nasty Twitter account?"

"Pretty much. You ruined my happiness once; it's only fair I got a chance to ruin yours."

"That's pathetic."

"Not as pathetic as you thinking you actually have a real shot with Dalton James. He's taking advantage of you, that's what he does."

"Maybe it's what he used to do, but it's not what he's doing with—wait, that's right, I knew there was something else I needed to know. How did you always know what was going on with me?

You knew about my date with Dalton before anyone else did, and you knew I was in Jamba Juice with Ellie."

"I have my ways. Are we done here yet?"

"No, we're not done here. You've been cyberbullying me for the past three weeks, and we'll be done here when I say we're done here."

"It's my house, Harper. I'll have my mom call the cops if you don't leave."

"Oh yeah? Then I'll tell everyone what you've been up to. I will blow you up, make it so everyone knows what a horrible person you are. You thought I ruined your life in eighth grade? That was amateur hour compared to what this will look like," I threaten. Whoa—where did all this come from? I sound pretty badass if I do say so myself, but if I'm surprised to hear myself talking like this I'm even more shocked to figure out that I mean every word. I'm not going to let Gwen push me around.

"Okay, fine," she says quietly, her voice so soft I can barely hear her. "I hacked into your phone. You do those check-ins everywhere you go. It wasn't too hard to figure out where you were and with whom."

"How the hell could you possibly do that?"

"It's not rocket science. Look it up."

"Gwen, do you realize how illegal that is? I could call the cops on you. I can't imagine how you could possibly even begin to—I mean, and you say *I* have too much time on my hands?"

"Maybe we both do," she says then, sounding a notch sadder than before.

"But how did you get a picture of me in Jack's car?"

"I, uh . . . I had someone take it for me."

"Who? Tell me."

"Ashley Adler."

"What? That's not . . . how do you even know her? I didn't meet her until high school. You had already transferred."

"We met at a party. That part was a coincidence, really. We started talking and realized not only do we both know you but we also both hate you. To be honest, I don't think her dislike for you is justified—I mean, you didn't ruin *her* life. I think she's just a basic bitch who wants to get invited to A-list parties. Anyway, I told her I'd pay her for any dirt she could get on you. That picture was the first juicy thing she gave me that I could use."

"You're sick," I say, genuinely horrified. "I can't be around you anymore. Stop tweeting about me, stop spying on me, and just leave me alone, or I will tell everyone I know all about this and kill your reputation, all right?"

"Whatever."

"I'm serious, Gwen."

"Oh, you're *serious*? I'm *so* scared." Her voice is hard again, mocking me. "I've told you everything you want to know. Now get out of my house."

I drive all the way home with loud, angry music blaring, absolutely seething that this girl I once called my best friend could be so evil. My first stop is the Apple Store at the Third Street Promenade. Let's be real, I don't trust for one second that she's going to stop hacking into my phone, so I do all I can do: get a new phone and new number. Start fresh. I decide to go all out and buy an adorable black-and-white-striped Kate Spade case to go with it (when life gives you lemons, right?).

By the time I'm home it's dark outside and I am exhausted. I flop onto my bed and text Dalton for the first time since I've been back in L.A.:

Hey bae, it's Harper, I got a new number! I had the craziest day, can't wait to tell you all about it. How's the fam?

No response. But that's okay, it's eight hours ahead in London, so he probably hasn't seen the text yet. I watch a few episodes of *Unbreakable Kimmy Schmidt* on Netflix, keeping one eye on my phone the whole time, hoping maybe Dalton will wake up in the middle of the night and decide to check his phone. I doze off for a bit, and when I wake up it's one in the morning. That means it's nine in the morning in London, which means Dalton is definitely awake. So why hasn't he responded to my text? *Oh, you know what it probably is?* I think. *He has no way of knowing it's really me. That text could have been from some nutjob fan who got his number. Of course he doesn't want to write back!* So I reach for the phone and send a second text:

BTW this really is Harper, not some nutjob fan who got your number. Really, I swear, ask me something only I would know! Your friend Roger was a jerk to me at Magic Castle on our first date . . . the bathroom floors at our room at the Kensington hotel were heated . . . oh, and we're both afraid of the clown from The Brave Little Toaster! See? It's really me :)

Thirty minutes later and still no response. I'm getting anxious. And, if you ask me, there's only one thing to do to distract yourself when anxiously awaiting a text: edit photos for Instagram. Duh.

TUTORIAL #7

How I Edit My Instagram Pictures

First of all, I like to keep all my photo-editing apps in one folder so I know where they all are and can easily find them. The last thing anyone needs in this life is to go searching for an app during an Instagram editing emergency, am I right? Here are the steps I use to get my Instagram photos looking super on point no matter what the circumstances of my life may be:

1. The first app I like to use is called Afterlight. Afterlight is basically a photo editor, so you can adjust anything from clarity to brightness and all that fun stuff. It also has a lot of really fun filters that I use for practically all my pictures, not to mention cool texture features, where you can make your pics look like actual old-timey photographs, which I think is awesome. This is also the app where people get those wacky borders for their photos; you can do a regular square border or a circular one or a triangular one, literally any shape you could want. Last but not least on Afterlight, you can set your photo up to look like a Polaroid pic if you want, which is a super fun throwback to the Polaroid era, which I sadly missed out on almost completely. So, yay Afterlight for re-creating the golden years.
2. Next is Pic Collage, which I think is fun for making your Instagram pictures look sort of like a page in a scrapbook! Definitely recommend checking this one out.

3. Now moving on to Lumiè, which is another great app for light effects. Once you pick a photo, you can add these cool light effects to your photo (my personal fave: sprinkling heart-shaped lights all over a photo).
4. Picfx is another great one for filters. These filters are a little more intense and severe than the ones on Afterlight, so this is the app you want if you're going for a dramatic effect with your Instagram photos. Picfx has a lot of cool extra features for creating a vintage, rainbowy, prismatic, or even pixilated look. The sky's the limit with this one, folks.
5. Next is PicFrame. I'm super obsessed with frames for my Instagram pictures. I think they add extra flare and help my pics stand out from all the others. There are basically a million unique frames to choose from that are all really dope and provide tons of variety.
6. Then I have Mirrorgram, which I use for flipping my pictures so that I have the original photo and its mirror image side by side. It shows you the side-by-side images as you're actually taking the photo, so you don't need to manually flip or arrange the two different mirrors once the photo is taken. One step, done and done. You can also just upload a photo (instead of taking a picture then and there), and this app will mirrorize it for you! (Pretty sure "mirrorize" isn't a word, but it's fun, right?)
7. If you're in the mood for even fancier frame options, try Diptic!
8. A really cool app that not a lot of people use is Over, which I use to write text over my photos before posting them. You can write whatever you want, play around with the fonts and sizes, and just have fun with it!

9. So there's Over and then there's Layover—have you heard of it?! I didn't think so, most people don't know about this gem. Layover allows you to layer one picture on top of another picture. SAY WHAT?! It's pretty cool if you want to layer quotes over your photos; you can select a photo and a quote and the app will blend them together for you in a number of interesting ways.

You may think these are waaaaay more editing apps than necessary, but I promise it's all worth it to get the perfect Instagram photos. All you really have to do is download these helpful little apps and play around with them. Have fun!

You are my everything goals.

Lots of love, Harper

CHAPTER 12

It Was Nothing and She Was a Nobody

The next day after school I head right back to my bed and paint my nails, each one a different neon color. This is a weak distraction from my troubles—namely, that it's been about fifteen hours since I texted Dalton and he still hasn't responded. I know he's in New York by now getting ready for his appearance on *The Tonight Show,* and I know that must be a stressful thing to prepare for, but can't he take just one little second to respond to me? There's no way he's that busy or that stressed out. He's not even an easily stressed-out kind of person! I don't *want* to be the kind of girlfriend who waits around for her boyfriend to text, but he's not giving me much of an option, now is he?

I keep myself busy with this and that as the night drags on, telling myself no, I will not be tuning in to watch Dalton on television. Yet somehow, as soon as the clock strikes 11:34 p.m., I turn on the TV and scroll to NBC for *The Tonight Show*. Thank God for dating a famous guy—if he shows up for Fallon, I at least know he's still alive. What do girlfriends of nonfamous guys do when they're worried their boyfriends have gotten hit by a truck or something?

Jimmy does his monologue, but I'm too tense to laugh. When Dalton comes out with a fresh haircut and an enchantingly bright smile, I sigh a deep sigh of relief. Maybe he lost his phone, but he's alive, he's definitely alive. The audience goes wild.

"Welcome, Dalton James! Thanks for joining us, buddy," Fallon says as Dalton sits down in that big gray chair that always looks so comfy.

"It's great to be here, Jimmy. As always." There's that hypnotically smooth British voice I love so much. Hashtag swooning.

"Yes, as always. I think it's your . . . fourth time here?"

"Fifth."

"Fifth, that's what I said—pay attention, Dalton." Laughter, laughter. "So obviously we want to hear you talk about *Phantasm*, the fifth and newest in the *Sacred* series, but before we jump into all that, the fans are dying to know, and I gotta ask: Who is this babe you've been seen out on the town with? Seems like it's getting serious and we still don't know who she is."

Eeeee! That's me! Jimmy Fallon is on TV talking about little old me!

"Oh, that. No, that's over, actually. And it was just a fling, nothing serious. I mean, she's not a serious girl anyway. She's just one of those YouTubers; they're pretty much the least interesting people in the entertainment industry. If you can even call what they do 'entertainment.' It was nothing and she was a nobody."

Wait, what? My face falls and my heart does a staccato beat out of my chest.

It was nothing and she was a nobody.

I literally can't believe what I've just heard. I must be imagining this. I *have* to be imagining this.

"Whoa, that's pretty harsh," Jimmy says just before I slam my finger against the off button.

In a tingling, light-headed, out-of-body state, I grab my phone. It's hard to steady my trembling fingers as I clumsily bang out on the touch pad:

What the hell is going on? Why the HELL would you say that about me?

This time he writes back within thirty minutes:

You kissed some other guy. You cheated on me. I saw the photo. We're over. Don't contact me again.

My heart drops to my stomach, and for a moment I'm certain I'm going to faint. Maybe even die. It feels like I've been smacked in the face with a pile of bricks. *This can't be happening, this can't be happening*, I think over and over while the world spins around me, crumbling. I feel the rug being pulled out from underneath me, and suddenly I'm standing on nothing. I'm falling into this vast darkness endlessly, and I don't think I'll ever stop.

I throw my phone across the room. I have to get those words

as far away from me as I possibly can. The wall opposite my bed doesn't feel far enough. I get under my blankets and hide from the world, hot tears pouring down my cheeks. I can't tell if I'm hiding because of my shame or because of my anger at the world for turning its back on me. Gwen was right: this thing with Dalton could never last. Maybe what we had was real, but he's written me off now. It's all over.

Gwen, I think then from beneath a pile of satin blends and down feathers. This is her fault. She tweeted that photo. Sure, Ashley took it, but it was Gwen who put it out into the world. What an evil bitch. She wanted to ruin my life? Well, she did, she ruined it good. If it weren't for stupid Gwen, everything would still be fine, Dalton would still want to be with me; he'd know I'm a loyal person and not some cheater.

Okay, I think, stay calm, this is good, all I have to do is explain the whole thing to him. Once he understands the situation and that I did NOT kiss Jack, he'll forgive me. He has to.

I haul myself out of bed to retrieve my poor little phone from across the room. Unlike my heart, the damage done to my brand-new phone is minimal. I'm about to begin my explanation to Dalton when I see his text again and it hits me: He didn't even reach out to me to find out if the picture was real. It could have been 100 percent fake—people doctor photos all the time—but he didn't bother to ask me about it. That means he doesn't trust me to tell him the truth, he didn't care enough to figure out the truth, or he was looking for an excuse to dump me. Either that or he's just a moron. I don't like any of these options. And what's more: without asking me if the photo was real, he went on national television and actively, intentionally went out of his way to hit me where it hurts. He knew I'd be watching and he knew how much it would sting to be called those things on national television. What an asshole!

My devastation morphs into anger. Anger at Dalton for using my insecurities to hit me where it hurts, but also anger at Gwen for deviously taking me down, and anger at Jack for never telling me how he felt back in junior high, and for even suggesting we go to Ben & Jerry's. I'm angry at Ben & Jerry's and Triple A and my car battery and Twitter and *Pretty Little Liars* and myself. The anger swirls hot in my head and then switches back to devastating sadness. These are too many emotions to be feeling all at once. I can't handle this on my own. There's only one person who can help me now.

"MOM!!" I scream at the top of my lungs, and in seconds she's by my side.

My mom, who is a literal angel, brings me a pint of mint chocolate cookie ice cream and sits with me on my bed while I cry out the whole story from beginning to end.

"Honey," she croons as she rubs my back in small, soothing circles, like she used to do when I was little and would get sick. "Why didn't you tell me you were being cyberbullied?"

"I didn't think it was a big deal." I sniffle. "I didn't think it would turn into anything."

"You should never keep that sort of thing to yourself. No one should have to deal with bullies alone."

"I'm just so disappointed, Mom. He wasn't who I thought he was at all. He wasn't a jerk, he really wasn't."

"How people act when they're hurt is an important indicator of who they are," she says sagely. "It's just a good thing this happened so early on, before you gave away a big part of your life to him."

"I guess you're right. But I was so excited about our relationship, and now I just feel like I have nothing to look forward to."

"I can think of one thing you have to look forward to."

"What?"

My mom beams. "I'll give you a hint: you went last year and had the best time of your life, and it's coming up in less than a week."

"Oh my God!" I clap my hands, smiling for the first time in hours. "Coachella!"

"There you go!" My mom kisses the top of my head and leaves me to be with my thoughts.

Wait, my mood falls and so does my face, *how will I possibly have fun at Coachella if I haven't made up with Ellie*? My stomach clenches with panic at the thought of not having my best friend with me at Coachella. It will be nothing without her. *What if she never forgives me?*

I take out my phone and type:

Ellie, can I please, PLEASE talk to you? I can't begin to tell you how sorry I am.

To my absolute horror, she writes back instantly:

Well, that works out well, because I can't begin to listen.

TUTORIAL #8

What to Wear to a Music Festival

I don't know about you guys, but I want to go to tons of music festivals this year, the very most exciting one of course being COACHELLA!! Sometimes it can be kinda overwhelming trying to think up the perfect outfits to wear to these festivals, so I thought I'd help y'all out by giving you some ideas!

1. Outfit number uno is a cute red dress from Urban Outfitters that's pretty short and has a cool white flower sort of bandana pattern on it. I'd pair it with a white lace choker and a bunch of bracelets, a suede hat, and boots from Forever 21. The key to all these outfits is going to be lots of layers. Layer on as much jewelry and as many other accessories you can think of, because that's what pulls the whole outfit together.
2. The majority of music festivals are going to be really hot, so sometimes it's a good idea to just wear a bathing suit top with some high-waisted shorts and again, accessories! Try a wraparound headband or an upper arm bracelet, that sort of thing. Bonus points for flash tattoos!
3. Outfit number three is one of my favorites because it's super girlie and I can be pretty girlie sometimes. It's a white crop top/peasant shirt hybrid sort of thing that hangs off the shoulders, paired with some layered necklaces, a fringed purse, some booties, sunglasses, and you're good to go!

4. This next one may actually be my favorite: high-waisted denim shorts with a pastel crop top and a really cute fringe suede vest layered on top. When it comes to accessories for this outfit, I would tie a bandana around my neck or my arm or even in my hair—they're super cute and an interesting alternative to jewelry.
5. Last but so very not least is a lilac-toned maxi dress with muted pink vertical stripes, black booties, and a flower crown, because what's a music festival without a flower crown?

If you're going to any festivals this year, I hope you steal some of my outfit ideas and have the most fun ever!

You're my everything goals.

Lots of love, Harper

CHAPTER 13

King Kong vs. Mighty Joe Young vs. Man Bun

Disneyland is great, I love Disneyland, don't get me wrong, but it is not the happiest place on earth. The happiest place on earth, IMHO, is COACHELLA.

Or maybe it's Disneyland. No, it's Coachella. No, wait, Disneyland? Ugh, so hard to decide.

Anyway, as heartbroken as I am over the whole Dalton thing, I just know heading to the desert for a weekend of music and parties will cheer me up at least a little bit. There's really nothing like dancing your woes away. Really, you should try it.

The lineup this year is so exciting: M83 and Purity Ring and Guns N' Roses and Robert DeLong and Sia and CHVRCHES and Flume and the Chainsmokers and Ice Cube! And that's just the beginning! I'm so pumped up about it that for almost a whole hour I forget to be miserable about losing both my best friend and my boyfriend in the span of one week.

For day one I dress myself in denim shorts and a bikini top

layered with a suede fringe vest, then tie a blue bandana in my hair and hit the Coachella field with Natalie and Andrea, two fellow YouTubers whom I used to hang out with before I met Ellie. It's not that I stopped wanting to hang out with them, it's just that when I met Ellie we clicked so much that the idea of spending time with anyone else suddenly seemed like a lot less fun. God, I am the worst. She did nothing wrong and I attacked her, accused her of betrayal. If I were her, I'd never speak to me again. The thought brings me to the verge of tears.

"Whoa, Harper, are you okay?" Natalie asks from beneath her fashionably oversize flower crown. It's three in the afternoon and the sun is hot as we head to the Outdoor Theatre to see Robert DeLong.

"What?" I blink a couple of times and thank God for my waterproof mascara. "I'm fine."

"Forget about him, BB." Andrea, who is a tiny pixie of a girl, grips my shoulders and leverages herself onto me in a piggyback situation. "That guy's an idiot. He's mad because he thought you kissed another guy? Do you know how many girls he actually kissed while he was dating Jade Taylor?"

"No."

"Me either," Andrea admits. "But that's beside the point. The point is, it had to have been a lot, and he's a total hypocrite for breaking up with you over some alleged kiss."

"But I *didn't kiss anyone*. Ugh, it's just so—no, you know what, it doesn't matter. That's not even what I'm sad about."

"Then what's the matter?" Natalie asks, sounding slightly irked, like I'm threatening to ruin her fun and she's in no mood for it.

"Nothing, nothing." I brush it all off. "We're at Coachella, aka paradise. Nothing is wrong when you're at Coachella."

"Atta girl, leave your troubles at the door." She whoops appreciatively and grins.

"Are we gonna be brave enough to ride the Ferris wheel this year?" asks Andrea, hopping off my back. The Ferris wheel in question is the third largest in the world, after the London Eye and Le Grande Roue de Paris. So, thanks but no thanks.

"Mayyybeeee," Natalie says.

"Not in a million years," I say at the same time.

"Oh, come on, we'll regret it if we never give it a shot!" Andrea insists. *That's exactly what Ellie would say,* I think to myself, getting sad again.

"We'll regret it even more if we're on it when Mighty Joe Young decides to stomp over Coachella grounds and angrily knock us over," I counter, feeling pretty satisfied with my argument.

"Who the hell is Mighty Joe Young?" Natalie asks.

"He was a giant gorilla," I explain very matter-of-factly.

"In real life?" Natalie is skeptical.

"No, dummy," I laugh. "From a movie."

"Wasn't that King Kong?" This from Andrea.

"He was a different giant gorilla."

"There were two giant gorillas? What's the difference?"

I shrug. "I dunno. King Kong climbed to the top of the Empire State Building and Mighty Joe Young climbed a giant Ferris wheel. I think Mighty Joe Young was just a nineties knock-off."

"Whoa. Why does nobody ever talk about this?" Natalie's eyes are wide and full of wonder, as if we've just made a profound discovery. I know this seems like the most ridiculous conversation ever, but it is the type of conversation most appropriate for Coachella. That's part of what makes it such a magical place. About *one hundred thousand* times less magical when you're missing your best friend, of course.

By sunset on Saturday, my legs are so sore they feel like they're about to buckle underneath me at any moment, but I'm happy as a clam. The combination of lots of sun and an endless stream of music really hits the spot. We danced our butts off to Halsey at the Outdoor Theatre, and then frolicked (literally) to the Coachella Stage for Ice Cube, and five minutes ago, we flashed our VIP wristbands and were let into the exclusive little quadrant up front by the stage (oh, the perks of being a YouTube star).

"Oh my god," Natalie grabs my arm a mere seconds into the show, "it's Jade Taylor."

I follow her gaze and find there in fact, like the pot of gold at the end of a rainbow, is Jade Taylor, looking more insanely fabulous than ever before, wearing an effortlessly cool white crop top, a matching skirt that sways perfectly with her body as she moves, pink patent leather flatform gladiator sandals, and a pair of big black Ray-Bans even though it's nighttime. Flaw. Less.

"Are you gonna talk to her?" asks Andrea.

"You *have* to," says Natalie.

"What? Why do I have to?"

"Because you were both hurt by the same guy! And also because I want to meet her."

I honestly have no idea how to handle this situation. My instinct is to hide behind a garbage can until the show is over and Jade leaves. The adult voice in my head tells me that introducing myself would be the ultra mature thing to do (not to mention the *right* thing to do), but when do I ever listen to that voice?

My two instincts are bickering with each other and I'm actually almost about to go say hi to Jade Taylor when I see someone much more important to me: Ellie. She's on the other side of the VIP barricade with some girls I don't know, bumping along to the music. Our eyes meet, practically in slow motion, and she looks away.

Just then I see a tall guy with a man bun (gross) standing behind her lean in and say something in her ear. I'm way too far away and the music is way too loud for me to hear what he said, but she looks appalled. He leans in again, this time to kiss her, and she backs away. None of her friends notice. They're too busy cheering as Snoop Dogg makes a surprise appearance onstage. Man Bun grabs Ellie's arm and I see her struggling to get free. That's it. I can't watch this anymore. A third and more powerful instinct takes over: I wriggle through the VIP crowd and hop the barricade into the general admission crowd (a much rowdier crowd, no doubt), then trudge over to Ellie and Man Bun.

"Hey, what's your problem?" I shout, wildly high on adrenaline. "Leave her alone!" Ellie is stunned to see me, especially since I bounded in out of nowhere like that.

"She can speak for herself, Superwoman," he says like a sarcastic jerk, sliding his arm back around her waist. Then there's nothing I can do to control myself: I swing my leg back and then kick him straight in the balls. He buckles to the floor.

"Come on!" I say to Ellie, grabbing her hand. She holds on to me and I pull her over the barricade and into the VIP section, safe from Man Bun.

"Oh my god," Ellie pants, "I can't believe you just did that."

"Look, I know you can stand up for yourself, I've seen it, but that guy was truly a creep and this urge just sort of took over. I had to do something."

"Wow. Thanks, Harper." For a minute it looks like she's about to give me one of her signature Ellie smiles, but then her face shutters over and she looks away from me and starts to turn to leave.

I grab her arm, desperate to have my BFF back. "Ellie, I was so horrible to you. I know you're not @ThatBitchHarper, I know you're a loyal friend and would never do something like that to me. I can't believe I accused you. I should have never questioned your friendship. If anything, it's me who's been questionable. If you'll let me, I really want to make it up to you. Please."

"You know what?" Ellie takes a deep breath and smiles. "I think you already have."

We spend an hour laughing and catching up. I tell her all about Dalton and London and Gwen and Jimmy Fallon, the horror of it all, and before I know it, we're on top of the Ferris wheel dangling over all of Coachella Valley.

"See? Didn't I tell you it would be magical up here?" Ellie asks.

"I can't look, I can't look," I say, my hands pressed against my eyes.

"We're safe up here, you psycho," she teases. "Let me guess, you're worried Mighty Joe Young is going to show up?"

"How did you know?!"

She rolls her eyes. "Oh my god, get a grip." So I clutch her arm with all my might and glance up instead of down. I can see Andrea and Natalie in the car in front of us, calmly taking selfies and eating their frozen lemonade. Ah, to be carefree and unafraid of heights or giant gorillas. "Okay, no, look down. You'll love it, I promise."

I hold my breath and take the plunge, looking down while I dig my acrylic nails into poor Ellie. Then I gasp: it's stunning. It's the most beautiful thing I've ever seen. Palm trees lit up in neon green and pink and purple; glowing orbs of light emanating from the tents, making them look like jellyfish; rippling shadows of people dancing projected onto grass and sand; dust swirling up, turning everything soft with a golden halo effect.

"See?" she asks again.

"Yeah, I see. It's incredible," I say, but there's a hint of melancholy in my voice that I can't keep out.

"What are you thinking about?" Ellie catches the sadness in my tone.

"Oh, nothing. It's just . . . it sounds stupid, but I guess I thought things were going so well with Dalton. I can't believe it's really over. It all happened so fast."

"Ugh, Dalton. That guy is the worst. I cannot deal with what he said about you. I mean, I was mad at you too, but when I heard him say that, I was, like, *Hell no, nobody says that about my boo*."

"Thanks, Ellie."

"No really, I mean it, screw that guy. Wanna know what I think?"

"Obviously!"

"Are you sure? It's kinda controversial."

"I'm sure."

"It's just, from everything you've told me, it seems like Jack is who you should be with."

"*What?*"

"Told you it was controversial."

I shake my head vehemently. "He . . . he had his chance. He liked me in middle school and never told me. He dated stupid evil Gwen instead."

"Okay, Harper, real talk: everyone is an idiot in middle school. You can't keep holding that against him. He's obviously changed; he's grown up by now. Well, not quite. But the point is, he regrets what happened in middle school. His biggest flaw was being too afraid to tell you how he felt. I think it's time to forgive him for that."

"I don't know, Elle, don't you think it's weird that he just decided to pursue me after I became famous? Isn't that sort of suspicious?"

"Honestly?"

"Duh! Obviously, honestly."

"Honestly, I think it's a coincidence. I think your getting famous happened to coincide with his growing up. I barely know the guy, but my instincts tell me to give him the benefit of the doubt."

"Hm. Your instincts do tend to be on point."

"I mean, Harper, you know him, you were his friend throughout middle school. Is he really the kind of guy who would like a girl for her fame, or is it perhaps more likely that you projected that fear and insecurity onto him?"

As the Ferris wheel turns, so do Ellie's words around and around my head. Slowly at first, then all of a sudden, what she just said resonates and rings out as the truth. This truth feels slimy in my stomach, but good slimy, exciting slimy. Jack has been there for me all along, even when I didn't know it. And sure, Dalton was mad when he called me a nobody on TV, but he couldn't have said it if the thought didn't exist somewhere in his mind. Meanwhile Jack has wanted to be with me this whole time, even when I really was a nobody. But he didn't see me as a nobody, because he's a real person. Ellie's right, he's a good person . . . and I just felt too rejected by him to see that. I still can't believe he liked me that whole time. That's all I ever wanted.

"Ellie, you're a genius. I have to tell him how I feel. I have to get off this Ferris wheel."

"You can call him when we get down!" She cheers.

"Ugh, stupid Ferris wheel with your stupid bad cell-phone reception."

"Let's go back to when you were admiring how beautiful the view is."

"I'm over it," I say. "Now I just have vertigo."

CHAPTER 14

Yours Truly, Harper

"Ellie!" I groan. "Why hasn't he texted back?!"

If I had a penny for every time I asked this question, I'd be a rich lady by now. We're back in Los Angeles, lounging in my lair, and it's been almost a whole day since I texted Jack:

Hey, can we talk?

And nothing. Zippo. Zilch. Nada.

I know sometimes guys get freaked out when they see that phrase typed out, but this is an urgent situation. I've spent the past year and a half brushing Jack off and I need him to know how sorry I am and that, if he's still interested, maybe I'd even want to see where things go between us.

"Girl, I don't know. Try to stay calm."

"Should I call him?"

"A little desperate, but sure. He's acted desperate for most of the year—you can have your moment. Plus you already know how much he likes you."

Before she's finished with her sentence I've grabbed my phone and pressed the call icon next to Jack's name.

"Hey, you've reached Jack, say what you gotta say." Beeeeeep.

I panic, hold the phone away from my face. "It's voice mail!" I whisper to Ellie.

"So? Leave a message." That girl can be so level-headed sometimes.

I clear my throat and attempt a tone that's casual and confident. "Heyyyy, Jack, sent you a text, but you haven't written back . . . no rhyme intended. Heh. Oh boy. Anyway, I was at Coachella and started to think and . . . well . . . I'd really like to talk to you. I know I was super rude to you at Ben & Jerry's, but I'm really hoping you'll call me back. It's Harper, by the way. Okay. Bye."

I hang up and scowl at myself in the nearest mirror. "What was that?" I ask my reflection, but also Ellie.

"Your guess is as good as mine."

"He's not going to call back. I was such a bitch to him, Elle. Dammit, we need a plan."

She furrows her brow. "What kind of plan?"

"Something to win him back. To prove I'm sorry. To convince him to give me a second chance."

"What kind of thing do you have in mind?"

"I have no idea! That's why I need you."

"Okay . . . Oh, I know!" She claps her hands together excitedly. "How about you send a candygram to his house?"

I stare at her blankly. "What's a candygram?"

"You know, like a telegram except with candy. There are tons of companies that will send them for you."

"Hmm, that's not bad. It's cute. I like that, we're going in the right direction. But at this point, I think it needs to be bigger than a candygram."

"You could hire a plane to fly a banner around town that says, 'I'm sorry, Jack! You're the one for me!' or ooh! Even better! Sky-writing!"

I laugh and shake my head at her. "Okay, I know I'm kind of rich for a sixteen-year-old, but I'm not skywriting rich."

"You could show up in person at his house? Throw rocks at his window and then proclaim your love in a sort of reverse Romeo and Juliet situation. You know, without the inevitable poison."

"We're getting warmer, Ellie, this is great. Showing up at his house is the sort of grand gesture I'm looking for and can afford, but it strikes me as kinda creepy and stalkerish. I mean, sure, he's shown up at my house unexpected, but I just don't roll like that. What if I—"

Then it hits me. The perfect strategy is to have no strategy at all, but to just be honest and vulnerable in the way that comes most naturally to me: in video form.

As soon as Ellie leaves, I sit down at my computer and hit record.

TUTORIAL #9

How to Ask for Forgiveness and Win Back the Guy Who Just Might Be the Love of Your Life

Hi, guys, Harper here.

I'm not here today with any DIY or life hack tutorial for you, because to be honest, my heart just isn't in it right now. I recently acted pretty uncool to someone I actually care a lot about, and I think I really lost him. Suddenly tutorial videos don't seem so important anymore.

So I'm here instead to tell him how I feel. To admit that I don't know what else to do *but* tell him how I feel. To respect his privacy, I won't say his name, but I'm hoping when he sees this, he'll know who he is and that I'm talking to him.

Listen, you, I hope you're watching this. I know there's a chance you're not watching and I'm just talking to myself and one million strangers, but if you are, I want you to know that the truth is, I appreciate everything you've done for me, and I'm sorry that I took you for granted. The truth is, I love you. I've never said that before, but I do. The truth is, I've been in love with you long before I knew it. If possible, I think I loved you before we even met. I know that sounds stupid—maybe it is stupid, but I don't care anymore. I don't care about seeming stupid or awkward or uncool, I don't care what anyone thinks of me. All I care about is getting a clean slate with you, and the opportunity to explain to you that I did what I did because I was afraid of getting hurt and thought I had to protect myself from you. I was wrong, and I know that now. I'm sorry it took your getting hurt for me to learn that.

Anyway, I hope you'll consider giving me a second chance. If not, I'll understand (though I'll be crushed, admittedly), and you'll forever be the one who got away.

Yours truly,

Harper

•••

CHAPTER 15

I Am the Sun and the Air

"Ellie!" I groan, "why hasn't he called yet?!"

Déjà vu? Yeah, same.

"I don't know!" she says from the other end of the telephone. "Maybe he's . . . sick? Maybe he hasn't seen the video?"

"He wasn't in school today," I tell her. "Maybe he really is sick." I'm driving home from school with Ellie on Bluetooth, my convertible top all the way up because it's starting to rain. It almost never rains in Los Angeles, and when it does, everyone complains like it's the worst thing that has ever happened to them. But I love the rain. It waters the thirsty plants and makes everything feel fresh and new again, plus it fits my #currentmood.

"Sure, it's possible." But Ellie doesn't sound convinced.

"What if he's like seriously sick? Should I go visit him? Make sure he's okay?"

"Do not do that," Ellie advises. "He most likely just hasn't seen the video. Everyone's loving it so far though, bb. Lots of nice, supportive comments, you should check it out."

"Fine. Wanna come over and keep me company while I wait by the phone?"

"Can't. I have to study. Finals are coming up."

Ugh. Study. I hate that word. *Fine,* I say to myself, if *Ellie is going to study then I'm going to go home and make a video about NOT studying*. Checkmate. I think.

TUTORIAL #10

How to Get an A Without Studying

Hi, everyone! I know my last video was a little bit of a downer, and I didn't even give you any tips or life hacks in it! Thanks for listening to me being all emo! But anyway, I thought I'd make it up to you with this exciting little video about how to dominate your classes without all those tedious study methods you've been told you have to use. Guess what? You don't have to do anything; you can do whatever works for you in this life. Besides killing people. Killing people is bad.

Unless you're like a mega genius, you won't get good grades unless you find ways to learn, memorize, and internalize the class material. If you wanna call this studying, then sure, yeah, you're gonna have to study. But I like to think of my techniques and practices as a brain-growing extravaganza and/or party. It is SO much more fun that way. So follow these simple steps and you'll never have to "study" again!

1. The first thing to do is make sure you have an organized study space. This can be your desk, but it doesn't have to be! It can be your floor or your bed or a park. The beach! An airplane! Really, anywhere. I like to lay out any supplies that I'm going to need, and also I gotta have my study buddy, which is normally my cat, Louis. Or, if I'm in a park, some wild squirrels. I'm not picky. I think it's also really nice to have plants around you, because they're alive

and make you feel more alive and awake. Your plants can be your study buddies! Little cactus friends. They're the real deal.

2. My next tip is to have a nice scent in your workspace. It doesn't have to be a candle, but I would suggest burning a lavender, cinnamon, or citrus candle, because those scents have been known to help with relaxation and focus.
3. Tip three is something I personally need to work on, and that is posture! I used to be a dancer and have amazing posture, but not so much lately. Make sure to check your posture! Sit up straight while you're working because it prevents you from becoming tired and unmotivated.
4. Some people say not to listen to music while you're trying to concentrate, but I just can't work in total silence. IMHO, it's all about finding the right music to accompany you in your workspace. For math, go for some classical music, because you don't want any lyrics distracting you. For English, go with some indie, artsy music. This is what I listen to when I'm writing essays, I find that it's great for inspiration. And for history or social studies or even biology (believe it or not), I've found it's best to listen to some R&B. Those rhythms help me tap into the part of my brain that needs to remember facts and dates and stuff like that.
5. Tip number five is a fun one! Chew gum! Apparently chewing gum helps you process facts easier and faster. Plus, it's freaking delicious, so why not?
6. I'm always one to put my hair up in a bun or ponytail when it's getting in my way, but actually loose hair prevents you from getting headaches, which obviously you can't afford to get when you have work to do.

7. Something that I do without even noticing is close my eyes when I'm trying to remember something. It's also awesome to do this while you're actually taking the test, because it blocks out distractions. There can be a lot of distractions in the classroom, so closing your eyes can really help you get centered and remember the answers.
8. Tip eight is to get your blood pumping! Before sitting down to study for your test, I would highly suggest doing a little exercise. It doesn't have to be some major cardio thing, just a short run or jog to help increase the blood flow to your brain, which, you know, doesn't hurt. Then you gotta relax and do whatever you gotta do to not feel stressed before the test(s) itself!
9. Now the best part: the test-taking outfit! When picking out an exam outfit, I would probably lean toward leggings and a sweater, maybe hair up in a bun. Another option would be a comfy little sundress with a jean jacket, something nice and casual like that. Just think twice before wearing pajamas into the exam room, because if you dress up and actually try, you will feel like you're going to be successful. But if you show up in pajamas like you just rolled out of bed (because, let's face it, you did), you're just going to feel tired and ready to climb under the covers.

Leave me a comment down below. Lemme know if these tips helped you get an A on any or all of your exams!

You are my everything goals.

Lots of love, Harper

CHAPTER 16

It's Always Been . . .

Well, shooting that video was fun, but it definitely did not take my mind off Jack. My room feels chillingly empty and sad. Everything is completely silent except for the pitter-patter of rain against the window. It's too much to handle, this silence; it's forcing me to be alone with my thoughts, and I don't like that. So I put on the moodiest music I can think of (the Smiths) and sit by the window, staring out into the rain like in any good music video about heartbreak, disappointment, and remorse.

I know, I know, it's like, how melodramatic can you be, Harper? And normally I'm not one for melodrama, I'm really not, but I had someone who really loved me and I was too blind to see it. Now I've gone and ruined the whole thing by being presumptuous and unkind. The rain starts falling harder and all I can think is *How appropriate.*

Then, when the chorus comes around, I have a small epiphany, a moment of clarity. Why am I being so hard on myself? I had no way of knowing Jack had real feelings for me, so how could I have acted accordingly? The worst thing I'm guilty of here is being a flawed human being. All human beings are flawed. So if I had love and I messed it up, that doesn't mean I don't still deserve it. I do still deserve it, and if I don't get to be loved for a while, that's okay, because at least I know I'm worthy of it. Really, that feeling is all we need to get by.

"Harper!" My mom calls my name from the top of the staircase, startling me out of my reverie. "You have a visitor!"

A visitor? Who could possibly be here to see me at this hour? And in the pouring rain? It can't be Ellie. She'd call or shoot me a text first. And if it was Ellie, my mom wouldn't have that suggestive tone in her voice that implies a gentleman caller.

Oh my god, it must be Jack. Finally!

I switch off my melancholy music and do a super-fast makeup touch-up, then head cautiously up the stairs, feeling completely unprepared for a face-to-face with Jack. What will I say? Will he profess his true love for me IRL or will he break my heart all over again? At the top of the stairs I pause, take a deep breath, and run my fingers through my hair for a calming effect.

Then I open the basement door, walk into the living room, and there sitting on the couch, drenched from head to toe, is . . .

"*Dalton*?" Shocked doesn't begin to cover what I'm experiencing in this moment.

"Hi, Harper." He stands up and holds out his hands, like he's just as confused as I am.

"What are you doing here? How did you find where I live?"

"Your friend Gwen reached out to me—"

"*What?* First of all, Gwen is *not* my friend. Second of all, how—"

"She told me everything, about how she's been trying to take you down on Twitter because of some stupid revenge kick, and how she tweeted that picture of you and that Jack guy and made it look like you two were kissing. I felt so awful for jumping to conclusions. I wanted to apologize, so she told me where you live."

"Why on earth would she suddenly change her mind about sabotaging my life and try to undo her damage out of nowhere?" I ponder, more to myself than to Dalton.

"I don't know, I only spoke to the girl for about twenty minutes. But she said that seeing you reminded her that you're just a human like anyone else, and no one deserves the pain she had wanted to cause for you. She said after she saw you, she just couldn't feel okay about what she had done."

"She's insane. I cannot believe she reached out to you. I can't believe you gave her the time of day."

"And then I saw your video and felt even more guilty. You were the one apologizing to me when I should have been apologizing to you. You didn't do anything wrong, but I was horrible to you. Truly, truly horrible."

"You called me a nobody," I remind him, not having the heart to tell him the video I made was actually for somebody else. "On national television."

He nods earnestly. "And I am so, so sorry, Harper. That was the most immature thing I've ever done. I was devastated when I thought you had cheated on me. I was so blinded by the pain that I couldn't see the reality of the situation. I acted like a child, and I'm so ashamed of myself for it. I would do anything to take it all back, I would do anything for a second chance with you."

"I don't know, Dalton. You wouldn't have said those things if you didn't actually think them, at least in some small way."

"But I don't! I don't believe what I said at all!" He starts pacing back and forth in the front entryway. "It's the exact opposite, Harper, I think you're the most amazing girl on the planet, and I'm constantly impressed with the work you do and the way you live your life so true to yourself no matter what. You're the first girl I've ever truly been myself around. The truth is I think the world of you. And the thing is, I don't even see people as nobodies or somebodies. I don't believe in that garbage. We're all valuable human beings and I hate Hollywood for imposing a system on us where our value is determined by how many people know our names and faces. It's disgusting, honestly, and I'm the biggest idiot in the world for saying what I said. I swear on my life I didn't mean it. We can go public, I'll tell the world what you mean to me. I'll go back on Fallon and apologize for what I said. Anything to make it up to you."

The earnest, pleading look in his eyes is almost too much to bear. And his promise is familiar: it's what I said to Ellie. *I'll do anything to make it up to you*. I meant it when I said it to her, and I can tell he means it now.

"You already have," I say with a half-smile.

"What?"

"You've already made it up to me. By coming here now. By saying what you just said. I forgive you."

"You do? Really?"

"Uh-huh." This time I smile wide, showing all my teeth. And in that moment I really am happy. Maybe it's Dalton's passion or maybe it's how lonely and sad I've been feeling, but I just get caught up in the emotion of it all and decide to stop thinking, just for a second. He smiles back, sighing deeply with relief, and wraps his rain-drenched arms around me until my shirt is soaked through and we're standing in a puddle right in the middle of my living room, mouth to mouth, heart to heart, everything warm and heavenly and right. *I am human and I need to be loved,* I think as we passionately kiss, *just like everybody else does.*

"Reunited and it feels so good," he says when we finally break apart, stroking my hair.

"It really does," I say, resting my head on his shoulder, looking toward the living room window, where to my total and complete horror, Jack is standing in a red rain jacket, face white as a ghost.

He has seen me kissing Dalton.

I have seen him see me kissing Dalton.

This is the point of no return.

"No!" I shout, almost directly into Dalton's face.

"No?" He looks down at me quizzically, one eyebrow raised. "No, what?"

But I don't have time to explain. Jack is walking away. I bound to the door and chase after him, ignoring the rain pelting my hair. To my surprise, Dalton chases after me.

"Jack, wait!" I call out. "Please. Let's talk."

"Talk?" He whips around to face me. "You were just kissing some pretentious British celebrity idiot and now you want to talk? I don't think so. I have nothing to say to you."

"Hey! I'm not pretentious." Dalton is standing on the front porch, the only one of the three of us out of the rain. "And we're kind of in the middle of something here, Jeep boy."

Jack looks at me, his face a pastiche of bewilderment and hurt. "Harper, what is he even doing here? How could you be kissing him after everything you said to me in your video?"

"That video wasn't about you, Jeep boy," Dalton calls out from the porch. "It was about me. *I'm* her boyfriend."

Jack turns toward Dalton, his face contorted in anger and his fists balled by his sides. "You're her boyfriend who went on national television and called her a nobody. Real stand-up move, buddy." Then he turns to me. "Is that true, Harper, was the video for him?"

"Well, I . . . uh . . ."

"It doesn't matter who it was made for," Dalton interjects. "I'm her boyfriend and we're working past what I said on TV. Now if you don't mind, we were in the middle of something, *Jeep. Boy.*"

"Screw you, you don't deserve to be Harper's boyfriend." Jack isn't backing down. This determination in them both is simultaneously attractive and irritatingly immature. "You just met her like what, last month? I've loved this girl since I was twelve years old and I'm not going to give her up just because you came along."

"Well, you don't really have a choice in the matter, now do you?"

"Oh, I think I do. See, that video *was* about me, and it *does* matter. Harper knows I'm the true love of her life. You're just a fling. So actually it's you who doesn't have a choice in the matter."

"Really?" Dalton laughs, and it's a harsh, almost ugly sound. "Then why was she in the middle of kissing me when you showed up out of nowhere?"

"I don't know." Jack frowns. "Harper? What's going on here?"

Yikes. It's a fair question. Why did I give in to Dalton so easily even after pouring my heart and soul into that video for Jack? Is it possible that I have major feelings for two guys at once? I gaze out at Jack standing tall in the torrential downpour and all I can think is *My god, Harper, how did you get yourself into such a mess?* Life used to be simple; it used to make sense. That was back before I had a following, before I met Dalton, before I knew the truth about Jack. For a moment I wonder if I wouldn't just prefer going back to how things were, back when I was invisible and insignificant, back when the things I said and did were private, just for me, and didn't matter to anyone else at all.

"Harper?" Jack presses.

"I don't understand what's happening." Dalton is getting frustrated. "Who was the video for? Who do you want to be with?"

"I . . . uh . . . I . . ." I take a deep breath, look from Jack, who's like a wet rat in the rain, to Dalton up on the pedestal of my front porch, then back to Jack again.

"Jack," I say. "I'm sorry, Dalton, but it's always been Jack."

Saying these words feels like falling from a cliff, cold wind in my nose so I can barely breathe. It's all too much. I close my eyes and wait for all the pieces of my life to land where they will.

I open my eyes, and to my dismay, both boys are still there. I think I was hoping Dalton would hightail it out of there and the awkwardness would be over.

"Wow," says Dalton, "I *so* don't need this. I'm out." He shakes his head in apparent disbelief and storms away into the rain. Then it's just Jack and me, completely motionless. It's an out-of-body experience; I feel like I'm hovering above the ground and might never come down.

"I'm sorry I said I didn't have feelings for you," he says. "I always have."

"I'm sorry I was a jerk to you for so long." I smile, realizing this is the moment I've been waiting for since seventh grade, the moment Jack and I confess our feelings for each other and the feelings are reciprocated and it turns out it wasn't all in my mind after all.

"So, um . . . what happens now?" he asks.

"Now I think you should kiss me," I say, feeling light and brave like I'm on top of the world and nothing will ever be bad again.

And that's how it happens. My first kiss with Jack. He walks toward me and slips his arms around my waist. I can't believe this is finally happening. He kisses me on the nose first, then on the lips, and when I close my eyes, I swear I see stars. I swear I can hear music play. For the first time in my life I feel like I'm exactly where I'm supposed to be.

CHAPTER 17

So Complicated

Aw, what a happy little ending to the story! My friendship with Ellie is restored, my career is blossoming, and I'm finally dating my one true love—what more could a girl want? Nothing, the answer is nothing. Sadly, this is not where the story truly ends, because IRL there's no such thing as *The End* (until the apocalypse happens, if that's going to be a thing). In real life, the world always keeps spinning on, and nothing, I repeat, NOTHING, stays perfect for very long.

It's May first and I've been dating Jack for two wonderful weeks when I open my locker to find a red envelope resting on top of my books. Inside the envelope is a scrap of notebook paper that reads: *Meet me after school at the corner of Fourth and Pico.* It's so obviously in Jack's handwriting. *Aw,* I think to myself, *my boyfriend is so romantic*.

When I get to the corner of Fourth and Pico, he's already standing there, waiting for me. He's wearing the black hoodie I love, his hands shoved in the pockets.

"I'm here," I say. "Is . . . everything okay?"

He takes my hand. "Of course everything's okay, weirdo, come on."

"Where are we going?"

"The beach."

"The beach? Now? I don't have my bathing suit."

"It's not like that." He laughs. "We're just going to sit on the sand."

"Okay . . . what for?"

"Jeez, so many questions. Can't a guy sit on the beach with his girlfriend?"

"Sure, no, totally." I squeeze his hand. "I'll just go with it."

"You won't regret it," he says, kissing my cheek.

Once at the beach, we walk almost all the way to the water. Then he unzips his backpack and pulls out a Mexican blanket. I burst out laughing.

"Who are you, Mary Poppins?"

"Maybe." He gives me a sly smile, laying the blanket out. We sit down and I stretch my legs out over his legs so that we're intertwined like a hashtag. Oh, hashtag, the international sign of millennial love.

He checks his watch.

"In a rush to get somewhere?" I ask, wondering why he's being unusually silent. Is it my imagination or is he being *extremely, un-*

usually silent? I start to get anxious. Is he going to break up with me already? Is the best thing that's ever happened to me already over?

"Nope, just checking the time."

"Okay."

"Oh, look at the skywriting." He points up at the sky where a plane is beginning to write out a white, fluffy W in the sky.

"Yeah," I say, "cool."

"I wonder what it's going to spell. What do you think it could be?!" His curiosity seems exaggerated, sort of over the top. I can't figure out why he's so invested in this skywriting. Has this always been an interest of his? By now the W has become a W-I-L-L, and the plane drifting over to the right, getting ready for the next letter. It's starting to look like a Y.

"I don't know." I try to guess. "Maybe 'Willy'?"

"*Willy?* No, look, there's a space between the L and the Y."

"Will yo . . . will you . . . Oh," I say, "it's going to be a question. Will you something. Will you . . ." Of course then I'm invested too. What's the big question in the sky going to be? We sit back and watch it unfold, until the final sentence is spelled out:

WILL YOU GO TO THE PROM WITH ME,

"Aw, so cute!" *I'm* a romantic too, after all. "I wonder who it's for. Wait, why is there a comma? Shouldn't it be a question mark?"

Jack says nothing, just keeps looking at the sky. That's when the plane starts back up again with the final letters:

H-A-R-P-E-R?

"Oh my god!" My hands fly to my mouth in shock. "Oh my god,

Jack, *you* did this?" I can't believe it. I couldn't have anticipated this in a million years.

"Uh-huh." He grins. "So will you?"

"Of course I'll go to the prom with you, are you kidding?" I throw my arms around his neck. "I would absolutely love to. Obviously!"

We kiss as the waves roll in, crashing against the shore like a lullaby.

"You know I would have gone to prom with you no matter what, right? You didn't have to do all this. I mean, don't get me wrong, I totally love it, but it's not why I'm saying yes. I'm saying yes because you're my boyfriend and I've wanted to go to prom with you since I was twelve years old."

"I know, it's just . . . no, never mind."

"What? You can tell me."

"It's just, I don't know, before me you were dating a movie star. That's a lot to compete with."

"Oh my god, please tell me you're kidding."

"I'm not kidding! Put yourself in my shoes. Imagine if before we started dating I was with . . . well, actually, I was going to say a celebrity, but you *are* a celebrity, so I guess you don't know what it's like to feel inadequate anymore."

"I still feel inadequate sometimes! I'm still a human being, Jack. And trust me when I say I don't need you to be a celebrity. I dated a celebrity and realized the whole thing was overrated."

"I just don't want you to think that because now you're with an average Joe you won't be treated like an absolute princess. Because you will be."

I grin. "Noted. Message received."

We kiss until sunset and then Jack hesitantly agrees to pose for selfies with me. Hey, if you wanna be with me, you gotta be down with the selfie.

"You know what would be amazing?" I say to Jack, who is now sitting on my bed while I sit at my desk, editing my latest video.

"What's that?" he asks, looking up from a copy of *Catcher in the Rye*, which we're reading in Mrs. Bulow's class.

"If Ellie could come to our sophomore prom. Do you think one of your guy friends could take her?"

"Yeah, totally. How about Bryce? He doesn't have a date yet."

"Perfect! This night is going to be amazing! Limo ride with my bestie and my boyfriend, dancing the night away like there's no tomorrow . . ."

"Then back to my uncle's beach house for a Disney movie marathon and vanilla ice cream with rainbow sprinkles in rainbow-sprinkled cones."

"Livin' the dream, Jack, livin' the dream." I sigh. "Can't wait to tell Ellie."

That's when my phone starts to ring.

"Ooh, that must be her!" I exclaim and practically pounce on my phone. But it's not Ellie calling, it's Dalton. My face falls.

"What's wrong?" Jack asks.

"It's Dalton," I say. "I don't know what he wants."

"Well don't be afraid, it's all good. Just answer. No big deal, Harp."

I realize then that I should have just kept quiet about who was calling. That way I could have just ignored it. Once I said out loud that it was Dalton, I made it so that I had to answer. Otherwise Jack would think I was hiding something. I had nothing to hide, so I braced myself and answered.

"Hello?"

"Harper, hi!" The guy has a sexy voice, you gotta hand it to him.

"Uh, hi, Dalton, what's going on?"

"So great to hear your voice, it's been too long!" He sounds incredibly cheery, especially compared to the last time I saw him, when he was melodramatically stomping away in the rain.

"Good to hear your voice too, Dalton. Can I ask why you're calling?"

"Well, besides just wanting to hear your voice and see how you're doing, I thought now would be a good time to start planning for sophomore prom."

"Um, excuse me? What are you talking about?"

"We're going to prom together, remember? Our agents thought it would be a great publicity stunt for you to take a big celebrity to your high school prom, and quite frankly I still agree with them. It will be an amazing opportunity for both of our careers."

"I'm going to the prom with Jack," I say, interrupting this nonsense before it goes any further.

"Who's Jack?"

"My boyfriend."

"Oh, right. Well, going to the prom with him won't do anything for your career. No offense to him."

"Well, you and I aren't dating anymore, and the last thing I need in my life right now is a publicity stunt. So, I'm sorry, but this isn't happening."

"You better tell your agent that, because I spoke to him this morning and he seems to think it very much is happening. He already has interviews lined up with *Nylon* and *Teen Vogue*."

"Ugh!" I groan into the phone. "Goodbye, Dalton," then hang up and throw my phone onto the bed (so that it had somewhere soft to land, of course; I'm not trying to be *too* dramatic).

"What was that about?" Jack asks, trying to hide his concern.

"Dalton thinks we're going to the prom together just because we told our agents we would a while ago. Apparently my agent thinks it will be amazing for my career and is counting on me doing this. I need to go talk to him, sort it all out."

"You can go to prom with Dalton if you really think it will be good for you," he says with preemptive bravado.

"Yeah, well, I don't," I say, grabbing a jean jacket out of my closet. "I'm going to go talk to my agent and tell him to call off the interviews. I'll call you after, okay?"

"Sure, babe," he says, pulling me in by the waist for a passionate kiss. "Talk to you later."

Dear universe, why'd you have to go and make things so complicated?

I drive as quickly as I possibly can over to the Beverly Hills building where my agent, Buddy Silvern, works. It's one of those very snazzy, quiet buildings with lots of big glass walls inside and shiny white floors and pristine gold lettering. In the past, coming into this building has been an intimidating experience, to say the least, but today I don't have time to feel intimidated. I storm in past the doorman and up three flights to the American Talent Agency offices and head directly to where Buddy's secretary sits.

"Hi, Harper!" she chirps. "I haven't seen you in a—"

"I have to talk to Buddy immediately," I pant. "Is he in?"

"Yes, actually, let me just see if—"

But she can barely finish her sentence before I'm knocking on his frosted glass door.

"Harper Ambrose!" he says, opening the door. "Just the girl I want to see."

"Good, because we have to talk."

"I'm sorry, Buddy," Lydia calls over my head, "I couldn't stop her."

"Oh, that's no problem, Lydia." He waves to her and closes the door, offers me a seat across from his desk. Buddy Silvern is a completely bald man, maybe in his early to mid-forties. He has a diamond earring in one ear and always wears a long-sleeved turtleneck. I swear he must have one in every color.

"So what's going on, Harpsichord?"

"Harpsi-what?"

"Harpsichord. Like the instrument. Just a nickname I thought up for you."

"Okay . . . So listen, I cannot go to the prom with Dalton James."

"What's wrong? Trouble in paradise?"

"Trouble in paradise? What? No, we broke up. It's over. I have a new boyfriend and that's who I'm going to the prom with. So please, if you could cancel the interviews I'm supposed to do about going to the prom with Dalton, that would be amazing."

"Harpsichord, listen." He leans forward, clasping his chubby hands. "Going to the prom with Dalton is one of the best things you could possibly do for your career. The publicity will be huge."

"But I don't need that! I already have a huge following and I'll get tons of views for making a prom video on my own, regardless of who I take to the prom."

"No, no, you don't understand. This is bigger than that. *Much* bigger. If you go to the prom with Dalton James, do these interviews, pose for some photos, you could become a crossover star."

"What do you mean?"

"I mean, it would be your chance to get taken seriously as an actress. Start having roles offered to you. You could cross over into the world of mainstream celebrity."

I swallow hard. It's been a long time since I've talked with Buddy about my long-term goal of breaking into acting. The truth is, it's been a lifelong dream that I don't tell a lot of people. I'm always afraid people will laugh and think it's ridiculous, tell me it's impossible. But now I'm hearing for the first time that not only is it possible, but also it's in reach. All I have to do is tell my current boyfriend that it turns out I actually have to go to the prom with my ex-boyfriend. I'm sure *that* will go over spectacularly.

"Oh god," I say, pressing my palms to either side of my face, as if that will help.

"You don't have to marry the guy, just have one more night with him. If your new boyfriend really cares about you, he'll want what's best for you and your career. And this is it, this is what's best."

I bite my bottom lip almost until it bleeds and wonder if he's right. See, what did I tell you? Nothing stays perfect for very long.

"Hello?" Jack answers the phone, sounding groggy, like maybe he's waking up from a nap.

"Hi! So, I talked to my agent, and he explained something really interesting and kind of cool. He said that—"

"You're going to the prom with Dalton, is that it?"

"It's not what you think, though, listen! It's the next-level publicity I need to break into an acting career. You're one of the only people who knows how much I've—"

"You've wanted that for a really long time, I know. Look, Harper, I understand. It sucks, but I understand."

"Wow. You're amazing. I really hoped you'd understand and you do. You're honestly the best boyfriend a girl could ever—"

"Hey, my mom's calling me for dinner. See you tomorrow."

And he's gone. I'm left looking into my phone, knowing nobody's on the other end. I never expected moving forward in my career would feel so lonely.

TUTORIAL #11

Ultimate Guide to the Perfect Prom Look!

Welcome to the ultimate prom guide! I'm gonna teach you how to get the perfect look you've been dreaming of. Everything from makeup to hair to dress ideas, all you need to know is right here! Let's get started!

First things first: makeup.

1. Obviously you're going to want to moisturize that skin, girl, and prime it! Do this before applying any foundation. I'm using my go-to Covergirl 3-in-1, which I've pretty much been using for three years now. Literally I've been using this since it first came out and it's perfect, why would I ever switch?
2. Next I'm going in with a heavier concealer to cover up any extra blemishes, because let's be real, we want our skin to look on fleek in the prom pictures.
3. Then I recommend using a brightening concealer to highlight various places on your face. Under your eyes, tip of your nose, anywhere that you want to look super awake and fresh.
4. If there has ever been a time to contour, now is it! I'm going to use this bronzer that costs literally one dollar (what?!) in the hollows of my cheeks and on my temples, before blending a natural-colored blush into the apples of my cheeks.
5. I was looking at red carpet pictures from, like, the year 2000, and celebrities literally didn't fill in their brows. It's like a new thing.

Not just for me but for everyone. I don't understand how people didn't do it before, it's honestly life-changing, and needless to say I highly recommend it for prom.

6. Now, let's move on to the eyes, which are the most important part, you might say. They *are* the windows into your soul, after all. For prom I personally am going to go for a sort of fluttery fairy meets dark mystery girl vibe, so I'm using this Covergirl Quad in Stunning Smokeys and using the lightest shimmery white color all over the lid as a base, then layering the second lightest color over that for a highlighted effect. The third color I'll be using is a matte gray, and I'm blending it in my eyelid crease with a large fluffy brush before smudging the same shade below the lower lash line with an eye shadow sponge. Lastly, I'm brushing on quite a few layers of mascara because I don't feel like putting on fake lashes. When you're not in the mood, you're not in the mood, am I right?
7. Gonna keep these prom lips really simple: just painting on some lipstick. I'm using one called Angel by MAC; it's just a pretty, shimmery watermelon color. Tada! Your prom makeup is officially complete.

It's Hair Time!

I know a lot of people get their hair professionally done for prom, but personally whenever anyone else does my hair I always end up hating it, so I'm gonna do it myself and teach you how to too! I mean come on, girls, it's 2016, let's take our beauty into our own hands.

Okay, so you might think this is kind of radical for prom, but hear me out: this year keep it clean and simple with a basic loose side braid. "What?!" you might say, "but everyone else will be wearing professional updos and elaborate Shakespearean-era-styled curls!" And yes, you're right, but that's what makes your simple side braid so perfectly exquisite: you'll stand out among the prom crowd as the effortless beauty. Trust me, girls, if it ain't broke, don't fix it.

Say Yes to the Dress!

If you're on the hunt for the perfect dress, look no further than Windsor. They have amazing prom dresses that are very affordable in literally every style your little heart could desire. Honestly, prom is the perfect time to explore your personal style and find something that feels really right to you, something you feel truly beautiful in, whatever that may be! This year for the sophomore prom I'm going to wear a rose-gold tulle-and-satin princess dress that is actually a two-piece (in other words, it's a fancy matching top and skirt and it's just subtle, classy, and gooorgeous).

Oh my goodness, you guys, that is everything you need to know to get the perfect prom look. Now go forth and shine like the beautiful diamonds that you are!

You are my everything goals.

Lots of love, Harper

• •

CHAPTER 18

You're Going to Be Fabulous

Prom day rolls around in the blink of an eye. My alarm rings and I hit snooze, then hit snooze again, and again once more, then reluctantly get up and go through the motions of getting ready. These activities are normally the highlights of my day, but now they just feel tedious. Why put in my best efforts to doll myself up if the whole night is just going to be a sham? And what are my fans going to think? Me "getting back together" with Dalton after he said those things about me on national television, how's that going to look? Aren't I supposed to be a role model? I glance back over at my bed and consider climbing back into it, avoiding the whole thing altogether. *This is going to be great for you*, I try to tell myself. *You're doing this for your career. It's smart. Don't back down now. One night and then you go back to Jack.*

At five o'clock, Dalton pulls up in a limo the exact same rose-gold shade as my dress, a cameraman popping comically up out of the moonroof. I roll my eyes, then pose for a picture. Dalton hops out of the limo and strides over to me, carrying a clear plastic box with an enormous pink rose.

"Um, what is that?" I ask, pointing.

"It's your corsage, dummy."

"It's . . . very large. Will it even fit on my wrist?"

"Sure, look." He takes it out of the box and slips it on my wrist while the cameraman snaps away. The corsage eclipses my wrist, hanging off on both sides. "It will look great in the pictures."

"Great," I say in a monotone. "Anything for the pictures."

In the limo he pours me Martinelli's sparkling cranberry juice into a plastic champagne flute.

"So we only have to go to actual prom for an hour," he says, excited, "maybe even less. Then we can leave and pose for pictures, take the limo to Chateau Marmont, where there will definitely be paparazzi. Is that good for you?"

"Sure," I say, trying to sound cheery. I'm feeling blue but don't want to let it show. I've been looking forward to prom for a long time (okay, so this is sophomore prom, same thing), and I can't let it be ruined by some dumb publicity stunt. *Chin up, Harper, we all have to make sacrifices. That doesn't mean you can't have fun tonight.*

We arrive fashionably late and the party is in full swing. The gym has been transformed into a winter wonderland with ice-blue streamers and plastic stalactites hanging from the ceiling, tissue paper snowflakes, opalescent balloons, and white, glittery fleece spread out across the basketball court. "Fancy" by Iggy Azalea is blasting from the speakers.

"So, this is high school." Dalton is grinning ear to ear as we stand in the doorway, looking in. "It's just like the movies."

"What are the chances we can mingle without being completely hounded?"

"Um, I'd say . . . zero," Dalton says as a swarm of sophomore girls, my classmates, spot us and run to him. They all want to shake his hand, to get a hug, to take a picture, to just stand next to him so that for the rest of their lives they can tell the story of the time they stood next to Dalton James. I step back and observe the tangle of tulle and chiffon and lace and sequin that is now surrounding him. *Man*, I think, *celebrity culture is weird*, then slip away to go find Ellie, experience a brief moment of peace and quiet.

"Ellie!" I call out to her when I spot her standing by the punch bowl in a turquoise velvet cocktail dress and matching heels.

"Harper! Hi!" She sets her punch down and squeezes me tight, a little tighter than I was prepared for.

"Are you okay?" I ask.

"Oh, yeah, I'm great. I can't remember the last time I was around so many people my own age! Sixteen-year-olds are actually kind of like aliens to me."

"Trust me, I know. We're freaks."

"Harper, you know Bryce, right?" She taps Bryce on the shoulder and he turns around. His boutonniere is dyed a toxic shade of turquoise to match Ellie's dress.

"Yeah, of course, hey!"

"Hey, Harper," he says. "Where's your date?" His voice is snide, like he's mad at me. I guess I don't blame him; I basically ditched his friend for a celebrity. I'd be at least a little mad at me if I were him too.

"Oh, he's getting mauled by fans. But he'll be fine, he's used to it. Where's Jack?"

Just then Jack walks up, and to my complete and utter dismay HE'S NOT ALONE. In other words, he's with a girl, but you got that, right? And not just any girl, but Jessie, also known as Jessica D. of, yes, the Jessicas.

"Hi, Harper!" she chirps.

"Uh, hi, Jessie. Jack?" I give him my best *What the hell is going on?* look.

"Hey, Harper," he says very calmly, "you're here with a date of your own, so I thought I'd do the same. You're okay with that, right?"

"What? No, I am not okay with that! My date is an act. It's just some dumb thing my agent is making me do!"

"Did you expect me to go to the sophomore prom without a date?"

"I don't know! I wasn't thinking about that!"

"No, you were just thinking about your career."

"So this is you getting back at me?"

"No, it's nothing like that. I just didn't want to come without a date, and then Jessie asked me, so I said yes."

"You're not mad, are you?" Jessie asks. "I'm not like trying to steal him from you. I just figured neither of us had a date, so we should go together."

"You know what? No, I'm not mad. I'm sad. It's fine, you guys have a great prom."

I've been at prom for only fifteen minutes when I find myself sitting on the steps outside the gym, my head in my hands. Tears roll down my cheeks, I watch them plop onto the cement one after the other. The sky is overcast and gloomy, June gloom in May, and I have goose bumps up and down my arms.

"Harper? Are you okay?" It's Dalton. "I saw you come out here. What's going on?"

"Nothing." I wipe my eyes. "It's stupid. We can go back inside." His hair is tousled, his collar has lipstick stains on it, and the sleeve of his tux is torn. Classy.

"We don't have to. We can leave. It's a little early to get to the Chateau, but—"

"I don't want to go to the Chateau! I don't want to do any of this dumb publicity stuff. It's so insanely fake, I can't stand it. Us pretending we still like each other just to get attention. "When your life becomes lying for the world, don't you ever feel like . . . like you're losing a bit of your soul?"

"Oh, boy." Dalton sighs and sits down next to me. "Look, Harper, I wasn't going to tell you this until later, but the truth is, this isn't fake for me."

"What?"

"I'm not doing this for my career. Sure, my agents wanted me to go to prom with you so I could work on fixing my bad-boy image, but I don't care about any of that. The truth is, I pushed for this to happen because I want you back."

"*What?*"

"I know I was a jerk to you, but you shouldn't have chosen Jack. I needed this night to make you see that. Yeah, sure, he's a fine guy, but you should be with someone on your level, someone who really gets you and your lifestyle."

"You broke my heart. You called me a nobody on national TV. Is that being on my level? Is that really getting my lifestyle?"

"I was afraid. I was afraid you'd realize you're too good for me, so when I saw a picture of you with Jack, I was ready to believe the worst. It was childish and cowardly of me, and I'm sorry. Okay? Sorry. Can you forgive me?"

"I can," I say after a few moments, realizing I've been holding my breath. "I guess I already do forgive you."

"Good," he says, leaning in. "Because I really, really like you." He leans in closer and closer until our noses are touching and his lips are seconds away from my lips.

"Whoa, whoa." I jump up. "What are you doing?"

"I *was* going to kiss you, but I guess you have different plans."

"Yeah, I guess I do."

I know what I have to do. I dust myself off and stomp back into the gym, make a beeline through the fake winter forest scenery straight to Jack, who is in the middle of dancing the electric slide with a group of about twenty-five people—Ellie, Bryce, and Jessie included. But I don't see any of this. All I see is Jack.

"Jack!" I shout over the music. "This was a huge mistake. I told myself I had to do this for my career, but I was wrong. I don't want a career that depends on me fake-dating a celebrity. I want a career where I can be myself."

"Hold on." He takes my hand and leads me away from the

crowd, trying not to disrupt the slide. But it's too late. My classmates abandon their dance in an attempt to eavesdrop.

"If I'm meant to be an actress, I'll be able to do it without publicity stunts," I reiterate. "I should have realized that earlier."

"Are you sure?" he asks, his face brightening.

"I'm so sure, Jack. I love you." My own jaw drops as soon as I say this. I've never said that in a romantic context before, not to him or to anyone else.

"I love you too, Harper!" He wraps his arms around my waist and twirls me so my dress swishes and swirls like the petals of morning glories opening to sunlight, "I love you, I love you, I love you," he murmurs this over and over, speaking into the hair on the top of my head.

Oohs and awws pop up all over the gym. The crowd claps and cheers, then quickly loses interest and returns to dancing. Jack holds me close against his chest as the DJ plays "Sweetest Devotion" by Adele. Out of the corner of my eye I see Bryce take Ellie's hand and lead her onto the dance floor, and past them, at the far corner of the gym, I see Dalton approach Jessie, who giggles girlishly and blushes. Delighted and amused, I watch them leave the gym together, his arm around her shoulder. *Good for her*, I think, *that will be quite an adventure*.

When I wake up on Sunday morning at Jack's uncle's Santa Monica beach house, everybody else is asleep: Jack and Bryce in the guest room, Ellie and I in the master bedroom like little seaside queens. Rainbow sprinkles from our ice cream party leave a Hansel and Gretel–style trail. I laugh to myself, remembering the fun we had last night, the pure, innocent, nonfamous, real-life-human-being fun we had. We played spin the bottle, Twister, and Cards Against Humanity; we built a fort and projected shadow puppets onto the walls; we sang karaoke, roasted marshmallows, and shotgunned Coca-Cola straight from the can. It was, no doubt, a night to remember. And the best part is that I didn't do it for publicity, I did it for me.

I walk to the living room and look out over the lapis lazuli blue ocean, glazed with morning sun, pressing my hand to the window. It's been a wild, unpredictable year, and it feels nice to have this moment of quiet and stillness to myself.

"Morning!" Ellie enters in her Blue Jays pajamas and a bright smile. The only thing that could make this moment of quiet and stillness any better is my number one bestie.

"How did you sleep?" I ask.

"Like a baby! You?"

"Same," I say. "Like a baby." I can't take my eyes off the horizon, which is crisp and clear, a razor-sharp line cutting through the ocean and sky.

"What are you thinking about?" she asks, joining me by my side.

"That I'm going to be fine."

"Oh, girl"—she kisses my cheek—"you're going to be so much more than fine. You're going to be fabulous."

Acknowledgments

I want to thank everyone at Gallery Books for helping to make this first novel a reality. Thank you to Zara Lisbon, who has proved to be an invaluable source of guidance, patience, and overall good vibes.

To my mom, for her tireless support, endless hugs, and unconditional love. I hope I've made you proud of me!

To my nearest and dearest BFFAEAEAES: my life would be virtually meaningless without you. Thank you for the laughs, the chills, the adventures, and the listening ears. Each of you inspires me to continue chasing my dreams, every day. You are my #everythinggoals.

Finally, lastly but MOST important, to my fans, my #Sierranators: ya'll, where do I even begin? From the very first video I posted, you've had my back, shared my laughter, my tears, my ups and downs, my greatest triumphs and failures; you're more than just friends to me, you've become my family. For all the likes, shares, regrams, retweets, and reposts—this book is my way of saying thank you, from the very bottom of my heart. I would be nothing without all of you, and I can't wait to see where we go next!

ALL THE HUGS AND ALL THE KISSES,
Sierra Furtado